(PSP)

# (PSP)

## Lawrence Ytzhak Braithwaite

alyson books
los angeles | new york

MANUFACTURED IN THE UNITED STATES OF AMERICA.

THIS TRADE PAPERBACK ORIGINAL IS PUBLISHED BY
ALYSON PUBLICATIONS,
P.O. BOX 4371, LOS ANGELES, CALIFORNIA 90078-4371.
DISTRIBUTION IN THE UNITED KINGDOM BY
TURNAROUND PUBLISHER SERVICES LTD.,
UNIT 3 OLYMPIA TRADING ESTATE, COBURG ROAD, WOOD GREEN,
LONDON N22 6TZ ENGLAND.

FIRST EDITION: MAY 2000

00 01 02 03 04 a 10 9 8 7 6 5 4 3 2 1

ISBN 1-55583-554-6

**LIBRARY OF CONGRESS CATALOGING-IN-PUBLICATION DATA**
APPLICATION IN PROCESS.

**CREDITS**
COVER PHOTOGRAPH BY HANNAH NAOMI. CONCEPT BY LAZ.
LYRICS FROM "CONCRETE GRAVE" ARE QUOTED COURTESY OF THE
   TEMPLARS. ALL RIGHTS RESERVED.
LYRICS FROM "007 (SHANTY TOWN)," WRITTEN BY DESMOND DEKKER,
   © 1968 BY ISLAND MUSIC LTD., ARE QUOTED COURTESY OF
   POLYGRAM MUSIC. ALL RIGHTS RESERVED.
LYRICS FROM "JEUNESSE OUVRIÈRE," FROM THE DSS RELEASE
   LEGENDES URBAINES, © 1996 BY DSS AND IMPACT, ARE QUOTED
   COURTESY OF DSS AND IMPACT. ALL RIGHTS RESERVED.
LYRICS FROM "DREADER THAN DREAD," WRITTEN BY HONEY BOY
   MARTIN, ARE QUOTED COURTESY OF CALNEK PRODUCTIONS R
   AND B MUSIC LTD. ALL RIGHTS RESERVED.
LYRICS FROM "LOVE RAT," WRITTEN BY GENETIC CONTROL, © 1982 BY
   GENETIC CONTROL, ARE QUOTED COURTESY OF GENETIC
   CONTROL. ALL RIGHTS RESERVED.

As ever and always to Andrew Allen

**All the brave smart thinkers and scrappers:**

Khadejah McCall, Janine Fuller (Little Sister's), Kevin Killian, Steve Doucet (wherever you are), and Richard Banner (Angles)

**Respects to the warriors:**

Peter Eicher, Lin "Spit" Newborn and Daniel Shersty (4/7/98), James Byrd Jr., Shidane Abukar Arone, Anthony Griffith, Marcelus François, Dr. Betty El-Shabazz, Michael Stewart, Matt Bishop, Junior Braithwaite, Joe Rose, Raybeez (RIP), Kurt Cobain, 160999aK, Ellsworth "Bumpy" Johnson, Sammy and Danny Ocean and the Rat Pack, Dusty Springfield, Keith Lauther, 020667bO, and Jeffery Lee Pierce

## Acknowledgments

Sounds and wordsmiths:
Slayer, The Pioneers, Metallica, Mayhem, Jackie Wilson, First
Strike, Business, Dennis Alcapone, Rancid, Skin Deep,
Street Trooper, the Arsenals, LKJ, Dropkick Murphy, X,
Skoidats, All Father, the Blasters, Dr. Skanworthy, Robert
Gordon, Jean Leloup, Cryptopsy, the Patti Smith Group, the
Hounds of the Buskervilles, the Maytals, Skanksters,
Pressure Point, the Lager Lads, Satanic Slaughter,
S*C*U*M*, Black Uhuru, Fairwarning, Chuck D (the rhyme
animal), Botb, Lyle Lovett, Blondie, Bard Faust, Bomb
Squad, Rickie Lee Jones, Exene Cervenka, Nikki Giovanni,
Wanda Coleman, Amiri Baraka (no sellout), Michael Pendar,
Michael Anthony Osbourne

## For keeping the faith, a Big up to:

Damien Echols, Jessie Misskelley, Jason Baldwin (The West
Memphis Three), Ric Irick, Michael (DSS Records), Robert
Nelson (Natty Rebel), Tobie Kraukenbuhl (VFS), *Red Zone
Streetzine*, Beck (Bek), Ron Depol (Russels Books), Mel
(Bolen Books), Nardwuar the Human Serviette, Heather
Patterson, Glenn Alteen, Richard Labonte, Stanley Bennet
Clay (SBC), Skater Fraser, Howard Gerring, Robert Edison
Sandiford, Laurence Roberts (Holy titclamps), Nick Boston,
Carl and Phil (Fritscher) Templar, Collin, Dodie Bellamy,
Camille (Megan) Roy (New Langton Arts Gallery), Hillel (MTL),
Paul "Typhon" Thind, Steve Noyes, Michael Turner, Makeda
Silvera, Tony Leuzzi (Gerbil Zine), Sarah Schulman, Gregory

Eugene Travis, Neil Meyer, Avery Brooks (this is the South son), Janna G, Lisa and Jason (Off The Cuff), Dave Hart and Warren Beech, Barry Clark, *Angeles Magazine* (RIP), Robert Dayton (Terminal City), Foufoune, Lizard, "The Final Call," JD, Makyta, Jamie, Noel, Harrlow, Justin (Lyle's Places), Jim Fouret, Frank (Crash and Burn), Stephen Beachy, J.R. Robinson (Ditch Records—great mom's cookies), lee (SoundViews/Do a Runner), Marc (Werewolf of London), Oikim, *American Upstart Zine,* Doug Herbert, db, Gordon B Sims (New England Hooligan), Luke (skin@gis), Angelo Moore (Fishbone), CFUV, Offbeat, *Redzone: Victoria's Street People Zine*, Mattie Richardson, the Upper Room, Michelle Lee Williams, James Earl Hardy, Kennette Crockette, Brian Bouldry, G. Winston James, Robert Gluck, David Mudie, the Niagra (RIP), Jennifer Finch (L7), lil' Ed Vargas (Mpls), Will Aitken, Wendy Morton, Cafe Mocambo (po), Little Fernwood, Beth & Natasha (Monks' Postal), Niel Wiernek, Luis (Wize Guy), Steamers Pub, Spence and Casper, Sterling, Ruth, Joy and Andrew, Ben Parisien, April (WHIP), Gill, Mike Josephson (Subway Thugs), Victoria Male Survivors of Sexual Assault, Skin Fraser, Graham Skin (the piercing boss and his sausage doggies), Cheap Thrills, Catherine Smith Jones, Val and Vicky (a&b), Dd's 'n wtb's, Peter Dube, Tamu Townsend, Brandon Jones, Matt Bernier, Adam Effingham Ackerly, Victoria Public Library staff, Scandels (RIP), Our Derek Falconberg (Victoria's own boot black), Cathy Sadler (Claymore Stables, Lancer and Doll), Jack (the Limit) and his thugged-out righteous torpedo—Steve

This book contains extensive author notes,
beginning on page 155,
which some readers may find helpful.

...this people draw near unto me with their mouth, and with their lips do honour me, but have removed their hearts far from me, and their fear towards me is taught by the precepts of men.

—2 Nephi 27:25

Who ain't a slave?
—Herman Melville

Another damn reason for the young to bleed.
—The Templars

...and the rudeboys bomb up the town.
—Desmond Dekker and the Aces

There's a little rat in everyone
Some ignore him while some think he's fun.
—Genetic Control

Cette chanson est pour nous tous
Jeunesse de classe ouvrière
Allez Skinheads chante avec nous.
—Impact

Now fellow rudeboys
come forth and let us unite
And deal wid one hundred
Or One Tousand years.
—Honey Boy Martin

# 1

Perhaps…

Quex waz lying on a beach with a sea infront of him for the first time in hiz life. All the otherz had scraperz and dirt and beggarz infront and over and around and to the sidez of it.

Jamaica—they got the coolest shit here. The tunes were sweet, so waz the people:

-You wantz somemore rum and cola, Doris-

-Just rub my back-

Quex took hiz hand out from between her legz and watched her rollover. He greased up hiz handz and went to woik—with pleasure.

Doris just sighed…what a pretty sigh.

## The Next Time

### Ready !

# Yes SA!

The state of active impotence.
The desire…
…but who could deal with the activity of screwing.

Sometimez you'd catch someone doing thingz
like walking, talking, sitting, and think—in
the briefest detailed fantasy—of engaging in some
primal screaming, sweating, and cabbin stabbin.
But the idea of tossing only bringz a sunken feeling
in a chest and heart.

These stomperz tried to keep it together
but too much…can't get it up. They were boichails
cool/coolio = over there then it waz Dumbdum, the
bootbwoyz = olbwoyz.

Check it! here it comez some new blood.
Headz spin = ratpatrols. Not tonight; not like the
other onez.
too much…

They had the option of going over the edge
with combz in thy're mouthz/shooting it out with
copperz—but thy'd never seen the movie. No one
told them it waz done that way.

This iz not to mek anyone proud. This iz
for revenge. Here they come: the Moonstomperz-
rudies-
yush = buffalo soljahz—not like the other onez =
not no
more.

But they got beatup. Too much! Too
'ard
 = inside.
Oh bwave new woild dat has such peopole in it.

# The Killing Field

Vodden took a sip of his beer and leaned back in his beanbag chair. The cow prints had annoyed him from the time Nalene had bought the curtains and painted the barrack box and walls accordingly//the chair was fukt and had cost too much for a sallyanne deal. Vodden never really had a say in anything because Nalene had all the cash//working in some ministry of...//dept. of...//office of...//some government thing. Nalene had all the cash but Vodden was a swot//his hands were callused from that dumb machine//his body was a wreck with that hernia and all. Nalene didn't unnerstand/his mates didn't unnerstand/his daddy/momz...wn'dneverunnerstand.

Scag in an abnormal mind can be a dangerous thing. It can mek you want to do things; sometimes violent/against yourself or maybe a chump or do crazy. Vodden was doing things he shouldn't autn't been doing.

The frequency he had tuned into had left him with a good plan of attack. It was all bass//chicken scratches across a guitar. His radio was snapping at him full blast with the message of pure crackling and pops//the station was btwn here and there almost to the end of the dial on an old bullet head box—screaming out patwa dubs—belonged to granddaddy. The only light came from the flicker/fluttering of the fukt up television set, playing havoc with his eyeballs. The flutters kept time with the baby's scream/crying. It sounded like someone ripping the lid off a can and scratching a chalkboard at the same time//but in perfect metre.

//it wouldn't stop/it won't/nah

-Keep it up-

Vodden was holding a Rutger standard automatic that belonged to his daddy. The beauty of a handgun, blk at the palm. Pretty fire/shitty smell/cracky sound/not as pretty as looking at it/holding it. See a soft target jerk back and slump.

Nalene never liked him to have it out/and with the baby/Nalene got even more ornery about the whole thing. What Vodden did when Nalene wasn't there didn't matter much/so Vodden did Vodden wonted/...'was his gun now anyhow.

The baby was crying but it always did that//lifting it always hurt his body. Vodden had opened a mag up to the video ads. He got off on the tastey couples. He targeted the gun site to the body parts he favored the best.

-A post office/yeah/I remember/that's where Nalene works-

In this room/everything was black and white and red/Vodden would dream of the Dumbdum boyz. Quex was the one that got him took in to get jumped in = all bloody and happy grin. He was Dumbdum now with no remorse.

He cocked the weapon and placed it in his mouth and pulled.

The cops/or feds/or something/raided his house once every 2nd wk. He lived with her = the overweight slutty cow. Nalene gets to work but it's a big shocker with what Nalene has to slob around.

//baby's dumby

He pulled it out and lowered it. Vodden targeted another body part/cocked the weapon and placed it in his mouth...

When his daddy died/he left him a trunk. Inside/he found 2 live grenades. He took them in his hands once and showed them to Flücky and Quex;

-...anytime I want out/I'm ready-

//Wa/wa/wa/you Dumbdum...-

-Shuttup/I'm reading here-

...He pulled his shorts up and left the room//there was a thud then another//the crying got louder and Vodden was having a hissy fit trying to find milky or something/slamming the fridge and cabinets...

-Fuk-

//It won't fukkin stop
//It won't fukkin stop
//It won't/it won't...

✖ ✖ ✖

# Ha, Ha Ha...

...going up and down that hill—over and over.

-I don't know, everyone's personal space, man.

My personal space is...like if you...you got to... It's so in me, that you'd have to be someone I want to be with to get to it, Ha, Ha Ha-

Flücky's yelping in the middle of Quex's truck. Yody's on the other side, near the door, almost banging his head against it. Flücky seez Sparker riding hiz bike on the road, down off further.

-Fuk, Sparker, man. We should kick hiz head in, man. It's not right he dresses like that-

Yody sayz;

-Sparker's psycho-

but Flücky keeps insisting;

-Oi, Quex, stop the truck. We should kick hiz head in. Why don't you run right through him-

Quex just takes a look at Sparker.

-Yody's kind of right, donchya think there, Flücky-

Sparker had a beer in one hand and a joint in the other and he was on fire.

Flücky seemed to be able to forever look without changing physical appearance to fit comfortably anywhere with anyone's fantasies.

He's yammering and yelling the parts to YDL's

*Skinhead88*—really loud and does a bitch about a vespa. Flücky waz a scruffy and noivus dude. He kept hiz hair at a length btwn these onez here and not the otherz. He waz a bit more posh in hiz selection of dress. Hiz sharkskin waz tailored to his train of thot. A special night it waz not—he just favored it sometimes—when he got a call to go out, hang wid the crew. Flücky waz a bit ridiculous.

-Youz guyz, you n'er listen to American shit-
He kept slamming the back of the two seats as grumpy Quex tried to keep a cool thot going.

-Pack it up, Yody-

-Oh, wow, I love this. I remember riding all day with my Momz and Pops blaring this-

-Your mom and daddy liked *US of Oi*-

-Hell no, it really pissed my daddy off somebad. I just did it to annoy 'em-

-Go figure…you-

-…he just, after awhile, slams it off. You know what it said on the back of the CD, when I bought it? "Made in England," HA, HA, HA…just cuts it (kills it) HA, HA, HA, HA-

Yody is almost swapping spit with the window when he says;

-Fuk you're annoying-

-Yeah/phukyou/hey, just watch what you say to me-

Quex reaches the top, again, where it's leveled out, and slams on the breaks—Indio = ? + Flücky = Van Cleef and $$$'s and more = he loses it;

-What Flücky?, or what-

-I want beer/lets get a beer-

-You drink too much-

-That's what it's all about/You drink and scrap
Oi/Oi/Oi, HA, HA-

-Me and Quex are little more than that-

-Oh/yeah/you don't wear no colours//the occult
messiahs/did you find that spear yet Mr.Bob-

Yody finally takes his face from the window and
looks at Flücky;

-Did you ever take a life Flücky-

-Let's go pickup Vodden, Yody. Hey! Quex! let's go
call Vodden and take him out to the pub. He don't
do too much no more since he started spelunking
that cow-

That scrubber had given him a kid that took up all
his time. Vodden liked working = blut and Boden. He
didn't cop tans on the cement beach or beg for
Welly//he didn't buy into Kahanism one bit. But she
was a pain. She did it on purpose//any chick that gets
herself knockedup in these times = is an idiot. She did
it on purpose/she did. Every chick wants a muscle
jacket baldhead for a boyfriend. It's to get him under
thumb and fuk her—beast like. Thy're not like shrubs
or spades//they got jobs and balls.

Quex Spun the truck out of the bush and onto the
dirt road.

-Great we're going then, Quex-

-Yeah, yeah, it's copacetic. We'll, call man...fuk...-

Flücky says;
-I hear she's part chugger-
Yody starts to holler;
-American Heritage-
They flipped a bitch and pickedup speed.
Quex nods his muscle neck.
Truck go…yes.

✖ ✖ ✖

You could get a bit of creeping moonbeam from
the balcony. I Edison headed for it. I Edison got a good
wiff of the smell of water. I usually get exhaust. The
living room was sterile, affluent, filled with stiff
German stuff and a couple of spookey African prints.
Lots of photos of fraudulent bovver dudes and
cammed out monkeys—unreal types. None of them
would know this shithead from Rhygin and I Edison
figured right 'bout this manicou and the Chubby's got
a stereo, no records/just CDs-and fukkin huge plants.
It was with the colours that all the light was absorbed
into the walls and furniture. The stucco starts grating
on my eyes.

When Chubby turned on the light the room played
with my persistence of vision/patterns remained glar-
ing over the edges of the tables and chairs.

Dark to light
Persistence in reverse
Glare

Like television.

I followed him in/right behind him//looking at the place/around the interiors. He had cash, like he said.

-What kind of music do you like? You hungry. Grab a seat-

He points to the couch. So I Edison go over to it.

-I'll put some music on, ah, maybe not-

He grabs a seat facing me. It was in this stiff long-back chair//not too comfortable.

-So what do you think of the place. We're here-

I just looked around and nodded, then I looked at Chubby. Nobody said nothing/for awhile//then he goes.

-You favor pussy-

-What, what do you mean-

-You bent-

-It's not important. I never really thot about it-

-I don't think so. It looks like you got good spirit-

-My friend Bragger said he was once-

-Not anymore-

-No, it's not that, it's just that he said/then he started hanging around it/then he was gone...-

I don't say anything after that. I Edison start thinking about whatz happening with Bragger/and then I lean forward cupping my hands.

-...peddled his ass, shooting up, leaving his needles around. He got real sloppy. Last time; he's wearing lipstick and 2 earrings acting strung out; he was strung out. Next thing I see him looking like a cleaner version of what I saw before. He even dyed his hair blond to match this old ofay he's seeing.

I see him sitting with him at Doll and Penny's. He's really moved up in the woild-

It waz there that there waz this blackout/cauze all he says is...

-So you're not a battybwoy, right-

-He used to be thrash-

I lift my shirt and rub my belly.

-Fuk, I'm starving you got any food-

Chubby just says;

-Do you dance. Would you dance for me-

-I had a boyfriend, once-

-So you are a punk-

-Girls have girlfriends, nothing special, even when you kiss. I've kissed a bwoy, nothing special. What do you wont me to do-

-You drive-

-Yeah-

-You want to give me a blow job-

-I could do that-

-What do you favor doing-

...like I'm some skanker

Like I got some sort of pricelist

Like I'm Bragger, now.

-I said I could do that-

-Kill me first-

-What, you dying of **AIDS.** And no, I'm not a punk-

-I like your boots-

-I wont to hear some music-

I walk over to the CD rack. I'm flipping through them and he's still barking on about...

-Kill me/comeon-

[silence]

-You got something to eat-

[groan]

So Chubby gets behind me and takes the CD out of my hand. He starts acting anal trying to find the exact place where I took it from.

-I think those boots...oh...yes, I think, Oh they look good on you. I like that-

-I'm tired-

-You want a bath/shower-

I Edison just turn and stare at him and say;

-This whole towns beautiful. I waz just walking around the other day. It's fukking amazing, man. Best junkies in the world in this town-

-Do you want to hear some music-

-Eventually-

I Edison walk past Chubby and fall down on the couch.

-How would you do it. Would you bash me over the head with a blunt object or asphyxiate me-

-Why are homosexuals always so obsessed by everything-

Chubby walks toward me. I thot he waz going to try and stomp on me. But then battyboichailz never do anything without a group involved and they don't like to get their hands dirty. That's why they have those

Skin wanna be/SA types = Q-patrol/marching up and
down the street. Well/seattle/youknow/wahyaspekt.

-I wouldn't call it obsession; but I learned to drive
so  I could get here without a cab. I have no
neighbours. Don't you think this a dream-
By this point I Edison had come to a decision.

-You got spare keys-

-No, just the 1's on me//…//comeon-

-No-

-It'll be a gas-

Chubby walks back over to the sound system and
starts looking at the music. So I point to the CDs.

-Those are nice. Not that I get to hear anything,
though. G-d you s-ck-

-You want to hear some music-

-Yeah-

-You dance for me-

-Sure-

Chubby hits a button on the remote and this beautiful noisy bashment music plays at a groovy intolera-
ble level. He actually did have some pretty good shit. So
I struggle to lift myself off the couch and I'm about to
mek like I'm going to move for him. I Edison touch him
and Chubby turns the music off.

-You'll do this for me-

-I don't know-

-You get the food/car/money. You can't park your
self on a cement beach forever jonesing change =
that makes you feel better. Kill me/you deserve

more. You hungry, want some music-

-I'm leaving-

...but I don't move.

-Where are you going to go to. I live too far. We're too far out, Eddy. If you kill me you could keep the keys, take the car: pocket money-

✖ ✖ ✖

I went to a doctor once. When I waz in school, there waz a guy that everyone thot waz coolio/hooch/snorky. He'd kiss his buddy Morbid at parties when they played anything by Black Flag. Thy'd dance around together and the girlies thot it waz groovey and the guys got kinderhard over the idea of fake battybwoy sex, then they'd target their pricks at the girlies.

He fukt me when he graduated. It waz on his couch at his parents place. They were gone that day, right. His dad wazn't there ever, because they got divorced.

He came in my eye. Then starts telling me about all the clubs he goes to. My eye waz still glued shut. He seemed concerned when he waz talking about his life. He told me to go and wash off.

[I had a tight ass] = he said that waz good.

A guy had told him that/he told me...when he waz walking home from school. The guy picked him up and stuff happened. He didn't get a drive back home because the guy got a little scared. He didn't think twice how scared anyone else could be.

My eye can open now.

I read in a Watchtower booklet that you can die. I figured I Edison waz dying, now. So I go to the school nurse. She's nice about it/really nice. Not condescending or fukt like a gym teacher would be. I think gym teachers phuktup more boys lives than anyone and now they expect you to do more of that shit if you wont to get off the beach. Gym teachers incharge of fukt over kidz. I Edison never found the meaning of life in a puck or a ball.

Sister sends me to a doctor/who waz a gym teacher, basically. He could of been. He just sat behind a desk with sliteyes/and got his helper to look at me.

-Are you bent-

How waz I suppose to know.

-You better check him out-

The helper shoves his finger...and then they take this swab and put it real deep in my joint...it hurt...it couldn't of been needed to do it like that. It waz real rough and fast...I waz supposed to piss after that but I couldn't...it hurt.

-Just leave it on my desk-

This nurse just gives him this look like she wonted to kill him and the helper waz considering a career change. Doctor just sliteyed sat behind his desk.

I saw a doctor once. Elie used to see them more/but thy'd put things in hiz head.

✖ ✖ ✖

I Edison shove Chubby against the sound system. He pulls himself back up...

-No neighbours, right. No coming or going. No you. You don't exist/never did-

-Never did-

-Right, Eddy-

-Never did. Can I take a shower. You wont me to blow you first-

-Just get it done, man-

-//...//Bragger//...//-

-Comeon-

Chubby opens his arms to me//

-Eddy, you're my mate-

-Fuk you-

I'm nodding and smiling, and almost under my breath, I say...

-I'm your boicha...-

I Edison slap him...

-What you like that-

...I keep slapping him. Then/I finally start to shove him. I start getting aggro. Chubby starts to protest and yells, 'Alright'/'OK'/over and over. This only fuels me, so, raging, I Edison shove Chubby to the ground. Then/I grab one of the pillow things off the couch and do this thing until he stops = no blunt object/though/maybe my boot...I Edison start rommelling the Chubby body and screaming...

✖ ✖ ✖

I can unnerstand why people off each other so easy these days. If you don't have the key to the universe, you can use a gun instead//either way/you've changed the channel. When I press and shift my feet in Chubby's car/I can feel the chipped paint on the porch. My cheek stings. I can feel this sticky wet stuff on my fingers. The fingers become my site and I can look just uptop them and see the cement walk and field and field//then I Edison look down and see Elie standing behind a little girl. She pulls her tiny fist out from behind her back. Her hand opens [slowly] and inside are pills—blue/yellow/blk = yellow 1's and small and a large green 1. Chubby said...

-People only come here to die...-

✖ ✖ ✖

- **G i v e** // ... // **M e** // ... // **T h e** // ... // **G - Ddamn**//...//**Keys**-

Then I just bend down and grab them and some pocket dunza off the Chub. I'm heading for the door, but I remember that decision I Edison made earlier, so I stop, find the kitchen, mek myself a sandwich and then leave.

What am I going to do with a fukking car.

✖ ✖ ✖

You always hate the minorities that are in your face the most. My daddy could never get anything perfect/not us//maybe our hair//but he tried/real hard on the lawn. Me and my bradder Duppy, we'd work on it for him/every other weekend/after winter. It just waz never good enough. He'd order sand and dirt/soil for the yard and we'd rake it clean. Then you'd get this chopper seeding thing and run it over the dirt. It dropped sesame straight down the line/forming a line in grooves.

Me/I...had trouble cutting the grass/once it grew. I had big bad allergies and I'd sneeze alot/so much/that I'd forget to see and run over the wire and everything would stop. But our hair waz clean//perfect cutz— fukkin near 1. He'd do it himself, like they taught him to have it in the army/war. Lasted about a wk of training then he got sent off. He waz 17 and lied to get in = This Is Your Gun.


//never run by the couch when he's sleeping.
(this is not a drill...)
//the enemy waz attacking
that war done him in good
           He never stopped
swinging
   ...but sometimes it just hurt/with all the scraping. You'd get a major rash. My momz would take over as he supervised. He made sure that the sideburns were all gone/just above the hair. My momz/she moved onto my bradder once and saw all these crawl type things running around. I have nightmares about them still. I keep my body perfect clean/because I see the other

kids//ah/bums/really/who hang out on the beach/think it's cool/it's cool to be crusty/big punk smellytypes/hollering at people for change and smokes. They got family and cash. They split every holiday/yud or not/to head back home to get new jackets and studs. I Edison get my own fukkin gear. I hate that shit that crawls all over you. They get under your skin and their babies are ten thousand strong. My momz destroyed everyone.

Me and my bradder figured that it didn't matter what you did with the lawn/it waz just crab grass we were planting/nothing pretty like our daddy wonted. I figure now/that they didn't sell the goodstuff/like you see on television shows/to niggerz who marry bAKRA bitches.

//it wazn't his fault = it waz the
              war that done it
              the war
    He went to bed swinging his fist
and cocking his gun.

✖ ✖ ✖

I just had to stomp that monkey…just t.c.b.…had to get out, get away…ya know?

✖ ✖ ✖

As I drive through the dirt road/barbed wired by

trees/flicker fluttering maple trees//the drive seemed longer and I Edison could see the sparkles from the bunch of water just past them/on the otherside/like the road I waz driving on/only I couldn't take a walk or drive through it. I wonted to see those things you see on postcards. It would be wondrous sparkles of the city. I pulled up to trees and I pull out a tape that waz in Chubby's deck and I Edison crank it. Rita MacNeil waz just ranking full stop. So I take a romp through natures pussy and met much oozy barriers of red where my boots hit the mudjuice.

Stream is louder than Rita, full force, through bushes—cauze it hits your ear—scratches you and rips your face...and as I get closer I hear rumble/rumble/ gulps and lopping of things and bits of notes from Rita. It's more scary than the city. But I Edison can the see the city/south/there/and the scrapers big and good. It stretches from the ground big/high. I'll place my kit there...not peddling my ass/nahno/no beggy/gim-megimme. I'll shine boots/plenty—t.c.b.. They favor them that way. 'Slow and Sure' Horatio/for Paul Hoffman//street merchant young/you and me.

✖ ✖ ✖

Daddy, I'm here. I'm here.
Yeah...I'm not goin...I don't favor funeralz...
I don't wont to...I don't wanna see 'im...I...
I just wonted to tell you that I can't even imagine or

begin to know what you went through...
I'm not a bumb...
I can stn on my own two feet.
Don't say things likes that daddy.
It's not right. No. I don't believe you do know.
I know you've watched everything I've done...had people watch.
I gotta go daddy.
Nah. Gubye...sallrite.

Daddy. I Edison've gone hunting daemonz.

# Down Pressure

...**most time** I'm just looking out for Elie and Elie for me. He spoke, when I talked to him, and everytime, he sounded like HR. I met him just when his parents had brought him over from this rehab boot camp in Texas. I used to sell him shit, until I Edison advised him that his crashes weren't worth the dunza he waz spending. Not to mention, that I Edison waz giving up the trade so I could start school in August. Which never really happened which is why...

...back then over there when Elie waz a stupid/dope head garçoon with Duppy and Prochain and Quex//Quex [Yeahyeah] **da don** puggugly scrapper of a spanking crew of big bootbwoyz and stuff. Quex waz the best tat artist in town. He had done 1/2 the town. He n Prochain even got to invest in their own parlour. He even did me n the The Horde. Not too much, though. People would talk—money don't discriminate—to a point. It's at the point, when that comes, that you got to take matters into your own handz.

I waz never a Dumbdum. I'm no friggin monkey. My head shines but deep down, yush, ...too rude.

...ah, it comes around—I'll tell ya.

✖ ✖ ✖

I joined, once-wot my daddy waz once. Said it waz the proudest day of hiz life. I Edison stayed enlisted. Even when they said we couldn't be who we waz...it's where I met Prochain. Prochain's fukt, buddy. Vods fukt. But that's cauze he left the crew for that cow he knocked up. But Prochain waz a scarey guy, man.
You watch.
You see.
Elie, man you lucked out, I said.
...and I tell ya...
...and Quex, he's cool. He just doesn't know left from right and everyone thinks he does. G-d waz really running shit—cappo and luey—luey and cappo. G-d'z bent did you know that? everybody did. But he waz cool 'bout it. He waz alwayz a boot first-the crew came first = army years. They came along a little later cauze I wazn't meeting anyone any higher than basic. They came along in the field exercises. I still never saw them. They were MP and infantry. I Edison waz Arty.

I met them at this base. I waz in my rack. I just got posted to this place, way out there. It waz real late and I hit my rack. No one waz there yet. All these drunken voices come in and some monkey yells;
    -Blkpeople are evil man-
    -Hey Faggot-
They called this guy Faggot. It wazn't his name but he wazn't Blk.
I'm not evil.
He waz, turned out—fukkin Prochain, man.

He waz just **Faggot** back then—a dEVIL retard…waz a mechanic but never could learn to drive = **Faggot**.

In the morning, when I got out of my rack, they found out I Edison waz Evil.

I waz in this crapper and it had all this writing on it:

# Watchout for Butthole Charlie

and:

Nigger this…Nigger that…

The base Sgt. found out how evil I Edison waz when he saw me. You can't tell by a name on a posting msg.

-Get that fukker off my base-

…and I waz gone with 6 months pay and leave. I ended up in the field again…later/away from there. Faggot stayed. They got him drinks every night, until they opened hiz barrack box and found nice photos and clippings—later.

**✖ ✖ ✖**

Before Elie and the blades...I Edison didn't do much caring for anything. He just fell into my chair one day. But I'll tell ya...

**The possibility of Elie** going to school without getting the crap kicked out of him/was next to nil. Elie would have to wear a crash helmet so he didn't get any further damaged. But it just trashed his crotch/cauze they aimed for it more now. So he settled for his head. Nothing was making much sense anyway.

He was condemned to an existence filled with dis-jointed signifiers//schizoidNigger/chimp/mallrat. The biggraçoons in the white collar hood thumped him blindly/mad eyed bruiser/detestation of the little retard. A nigger and an idiot is, too much, close to the truht than could be handled.

Thy'd wear ski masks or shadez and hankiez = colourz. Just like the music videoz. The voices made things clear enough for him.

They threw him down. He was circled in on and he could see/from btwn their legs = the fence and apts across the street. Thy'd said, he had sucked off the basketball team. Then a big boot to the head. Then lots of boots.

His parents never knew when he was around. Thy'd know if he was at school, most of the time, because the phone rang//principal or hospital.

**Everything was going good**/real good. Things were good and clean and nice like. He doubled the medication and felt better/and then Duppy came by. He was 22 = backwards that's 22.

Duppy's polite and soft/in the beginning. He talks about what Elie's got. He didn't talk about the weather. He didn't ask age/you could really tell by looking at Elie what he waz. He was little and pretty/nice and clean//no fukking geto chimp. Duppy was looking at Elie// talking real soft. He wonted to go for a drive. Duppy had a nice car. He had a nice bomber jacket that had his store shield on the back. Elie had bought some discs there. That's where Duppy really saw him and now he was off work. He could follow him to the park and miss that karaoke part at the local.

Bragger was going to sing that night. He was like a rock star when he was up there. Every note/every note/was right on/he was a rock star up there/but then it would end and that was it//bam//just another skanka.

Duppy waz supposed to be going to meet Bragger— head off to Tim's—get shit done and stuff. He waited for him all day outside the tavern. They worked well together/once.

It waz a couple of dayz later, that Bragger had told me, he had no place to stay and that he got thrown out of his room. He'd been walking for the past week in a deadman's shoez.

# Bow

The psych nurse waz trying to be peaceful towardz me while I waited for Elie, who had done himself bad this time//here a slash, there a slash.

-You know we really don't have any money for you and your friend Eddy-

Nursey had left to attend to this exchange patient the trooperz were carting over from somewhere. They got me a social worker to replace her.

-That's real pretty, those jars-

They were all wide angle/stretched and woobly.

-You think so, Eddy-

-You hide the needles now, donchya-

She spent more time trying to convince me to take Elie out of the state and stop being a burden on the taxpayers, than she did listening to what we could do with a boy who's getting to old for this checkout shit.

I Edison had my shoeshine stand now. We could mek plenty good stuff/green/to keep and spend/me and Elie…and he had a candle.

-I don't wont your dunza-

-It's just that people come in here and think we have some-

-People just keep coming-

I Edison rub my patch that covers that burn hole that was once on there. There are a thousand memories you could remember in a day and someone had stolen mine awhile ago. Then I met Elie, before that, I Edison waz looking to get them back. Sometimes I try and get it again. I Edison'm a strong guy—inside. I could take care of him and him me…jus got to get away from the govt and get back our lives. I Edison figured it wazn't in the worker's pocket.

✖ ✖ ✖

Elie figured he could duck into 1 of the alleys and clean off some of the gook that waz slicking up his gear. He saw a figure start strolling off a little too uncasual and stuffing something in his pocket.

-Bragger-

Bragger turned around and came back toward Elie. He had a garbage bag in his hand. Bragger had a rubber walk and waz a real quick stepper. His speech waz speed//chronic without crashing.

-Hey, Elie, so you want some now-

-Yeah-

-Good, cauze I've got to find a place to stay = t.c.b., right. El? You know what that dumb fuk Yanncy did. She got us thrown out of hotel, eh. She left her needles all over the place. Check ça! It's good man all rock. I got it off these lebanese. But I've got to crush it. He's such a fukking idiot. I couldn't stay at your place could I? Here look. Pure rock but I've got to break it up. It's 50, eh. Here, come on we'll go in behind here. I've got to break it, eh. *C'est bon,* man, *c'est bon.* Look at that…that's fukking *bon* stuff. I've just got to break it. You've got something…never mind I got it…-

**Bragger** waz squatting just a few feet away from Elie. He had his arms on his lap//wringing his hands gently/choking a needle btwn them/as he never stared away from Elie's beady brown eyes and the scar on his cheek.

-So you hear from Prochain, still? See Eddy, lately-

✖ ✖ ✖

You can't really go a month without getting violent. I Edison waz taught at an early age that violence is a weakness//but when you don't really have any other option….

-I guess he's avoiding you-
-I…-
-So tell me…-
-…Well…-

Wotz there to say…Elie's got hiz own way of going bout talking—if you follow him to places—it can get real fun.

✖ ✖ ✖

-**So he shuffled...**//Duppy's hand was holding onto
an iron lung on wheels = he waz once a great man//his
chest just filled up with the stuff and he'd breath nitri-
coxide out of his mouth hole. You could s-ck face with
him on the beach and get a shotgun blast of whirly ollie
head flips = silent trux sooper sticky gumball rubber
spheres over head-

-What's the matter-
Elie raised his head from Duppy's lap.
-What's wrong//is that all you do-
Elie took a big gulp...
-You don't move//bounce//give a little lick-
Elie opened his mouth...
-Do something don't just stick it in there...-
//and Duppy poked his finger btwn Elie's lips.

**The motor of the car** waz running, because it waz
cold and the heating needed to be on. No 1 was around
in the back parking lot, but there was a construction
site just after it and an apt building with the lights on
behind = Some 1 could have a telescope or good eye-
sight. Elie took a gulp and stared at Duppy.
-That was shit kid...-
He walked Elie down the street.

Duppywasspeakingsooperfast/sortofmadcrazy/kin
dapunk = but he's not...
-You're not fukking geto, man-

Duppy said he preferred to sniff = was talking about scag.

-Punk = big time gutter-
It's the best/Duppy said/to sniff = snorting's groovy, but sniffing is better/Pacho sold it/best to get it from Tim/Pacho OD'd last night = best to get it from Tim.

-It smells nice when you smoke it-

❌ ❌ ❌

**She wasn't much old.** The young guy [Tim] was lying next to her. The kid kept hiding under the covers. She pulled her head up and was looking at me.

Duppy was sitting beside Elie/beside the futon/waiting for Elie/to answer//he was gloating = my pet thing.

-So, how are you-
-Fine-
-How is he really/Duppy-
-Sucks shit man-
-Does he have anything worthwhile-
-Huh-
-Fuk it-
-Haven't checked/you got scag-
-Duppy/you've been drinking longer than he's been alive-
-She's a pretty grommet//…//Scag, Tim, you got or wot-

**She starts to say something**//'thy're all jackassez or something.

-That boy who chased you/used to chase you/bother you/at the train station-

**She sat up.** Her eyes were all watery and she had small tits\\but cute 1's. Elie wonted to suck on them/but Elie's no good at that//He was told = It'd be different.

She was smiling\a bit\\I guess\when she 1st poked her head out from under. Maybe Duppy and Tim and me could take turns on her.

-Cock slap the bitch-
-Yeah, he used to chase...-

**She said OK.** She never looked at me/Duppy/or Tim//even though I wasn't much older = but smarter//yeah. She had a chelsea...[...but she was noway real]. Tim got good hair cuts = it looked. Tim wasn't much older = than me. Duppy was showing me off//his pretty thing//pretty/pretty thing//all cutey.

-Get off her-
-No/no/I want to see this-

**He was a creep** but Duppy got off on it//Looking at Elie. Sucking on iron = fuming mouth hole//crashing head 1st on hard sand mixed pavement.

So I scribbled my graffiti on her back took a puff off the tin foil and headed for the concrete beach//and when I got there//I went = Oh Shit I forgot my tagg.

Duppy wonted to be a gangster of love = that's wot he called himself/anyway. You know he'd say this and try and fuk after he plied them with scag/shrooms/acid/lilgrrrls and jojo [yoyo].

So there I was//fukking like a savage monkey. Tim poked his head up from btwn her bloody legs...and I got my knees on her chest. So we go//
-Hey **Duppy**/why don't you get a **girl** fuk-

...and he'd dream//while she boohoo'd/sticky faced now//of a 1000 [1 thousand] skaters riding naked down the blvd as the media watched cauze he it wanted to = happen.

**✖ ✖ ✖**

**Bragger never took his eyes** off of Elie/who was looking straight at the brick wall/rubbing the palms of his hands against his knee/waiting for it to kick in.
-Eddy was asking about you/sometime. You want buy a pair of Docs-
Elie could smell Prochain. He smelled him shaving his head = Prochain blowing the bitz out onto the porcelain/wiping it clean with a harmonica blaring in the background.

✖ ✖ ✖

**...Just slams her** head into the wood floors. Tim laughed. Duppy smoked. He got her down/pinned good/ really... She bit Elie on the face. He started wahlin' on her. Tim came next. He kicked her over and Duppy passed Elie the rolled bill and tinfoil. Her hand closed.

**bLAM bLAM...**

✖ ✖ ✖

**I'd knew I'd treat him nice though.** I see him alot walking around with that Prochain nut. It was amazing Prochain could be with anything, he waz ego centred and a fukking retard. I could usually see them from eye level or from straight on. If I wazn't tying shoes/which waz a major hassle in life/but Velcro waz no better, it didn't last long and it slipped alot.

Sun stretches...

✖ ✖ ✖

**Elie woke up** on a park bench looking like a freshcut from hell. He was wearing clean, clean clothes and all hiz stuff was gone. It was wet and chilly + Stickey dew to his face. The wind would rack right through him. Then the sun would come in and warm him up a bit then it'd happen again. He'd shake and relax being completely manipulated by the weather.

Prochain's eyes were hard crystal and they were looking down at Elie and that caked scab on his cheek that looked like a bite mark. His eyes could go from sadness to insanity. They flickered btwn the 2 as predictable as an atonal chord progression. Prochain waz doing a correspondence crse hoping to become a C.O. He waz a lil'bitch working at being a player. He smelled like a junkie//you could get a whiff of him from a block...Prochain couldn't deal with the responsibility of someone elses feelings. He needed something to occupy his headspace. So he invested in a TV offer for Bob Dylan's complete collection/and'd smoke 5 joints a day and other shit. He was wearing this gray T-shirt//he wore it everyday. It read: Part Animal Part Machine/but he only owned 3 other things by Henry//a book of poetry/Hot Animal Machine and a promo copy of Hank's band at Woodstock, which no 1 really could take seriously, except for Prochain, who rarely got any joke. Even the 1 on his shirt. He had memorized *A 1000 Ways to Die.*

Prochain kept looking at Elie and figured that his headbracket had to be filled since him and that night before. Not to mention his horoscope, that day, said things were going to be good/real good/for him.

-I gotta go to the doctor-

-Yeah-

✖ ✖ ✖

Prochain pulled out the photoalbum from this drawer of Rhowanda boys/cut with precision from magazines he contained btwn plastic sheets. Hiz horniness was magnified by the beauty of boys//Leonardo DiCaprio and auschwitz victims stark naked/ready for him. He tugged to photographs of boys on lowriders in Slap and Thrasher/belzin/dachau/treblinka/buchenwald/all piled up over him in a pit/loving the desire of their sunken chests and bony hips. Prochain'd kiss them in their hollow holes and while staring into Keith Richards's smackdead eyes/he'd caress ethiopia and the soft targets of brazilian deathsquads.

## Tuffer Than TUFF

# "HATE IS YOUR LAW AND REVENGE IS YOUR 1ST DUTY"

It stretches from the ground big/high. I Edison tore apart that phukhead'z car in my grab and flee. I tookout the seat and made this perfect shoeshine stand. I'll place my kit here—t.c.b., plenty—not peddling my ass/nahno/nobeggy/gimmegimme. I'll black plenty of shoez. I always figured it like this...your average joe normal—casual—battyboichail—are peds man. They wont ya/when you're starving/on the street/they wont ya—it's all control. They go weekend hunting looking for ruffboichail'z. They wontz to be quickened... I Edison basically loseout 3 wayz. That's my opinion, buddy. I'm no obsessive phukwit.

There'z a natural selection in nature—those who r weak and unfit, get into that stuff, so they want be able to reproduce.

Fuk, man, I Edison see beaucoup/alot—everything. The everything goez from declaration to travesty. No one'z got a G-damn clue. A Moonstomperz a Moonstomper. You're in or you're out. All the bullerz I meet, blacking boots n shoez, that I get could say I sort of favored, never made it a career move. Being a

Moonstomper, a bandolous, datz a fukkin career move...I'll tell ya that much.

I'll tell ya the truht...ya know?

# 2

**A Smart New Harrington and OXBlood Rule o.K.**

Vodden and a chug were sitting at a burned down, smooth wooden table.

-I'm part...-

He names some fukt tribe that's unpronounceable. He reeked of beer/whiskey/and aquavelva. He comes by just as Vodden's finding a table for the olbwoyz. So this Chugger, spotting a dip into a possible pitcher, decides to pull a beerslut and mek chummychummy. The chairs are wooden and woobly.

Vodden was waiting on Quex and the Dumbdumz = to get a viddy at this wellybwoy. He also hoping that the seat don't give him sea sickness/or is the type that pinch your ass.

-Hey = hey = hey = could = hey....-

The Chugger tries tapping the sleeve of Vodden's flight. Vodden looks at the arm on his flight and sees a possible disembodied hand.

-...get a beer or a smoke off ya-

-Soddoff-

Vodden's attention was grabbed by the kinderwhores all over. They had those acme "Daisy Dukes" t-shirts on/and even by the breast/you couldn't tell how old they were. Teeny tiny backpacks with tampons and "**e**" inside. They didn't know what a fuk was. They let those kiddyfuk vagenbwoyz slide it up and down for a few seconds = think they hit nirvana//I'll take you to Valhalla. Niglets too//they let up there//1488 = I'll bash it up and holler your name before I pearly up your neck/sis.

-Fuk I'm getting hard…-

-Whaaawhatdid//ysay…-

Vodden thot about light and history. Vodden was getting a major chub while the drunken indian is yammer, yammer, yammering, yaddiddy, blah, blah, blah. A kinderwhore sat just upfront from Vodden//to the side//right//and he wondered if she could have cum just sitting there, pretending to listen to the music and when she crossed and uncrossed her legs = she'd get wet and cum. How would you light it in there = use shadow for texture/in his head/so he could taste it = poke a finger print on the linings. He'd toss light up into it/get it to shoot down and narrow his face to get eye level with the top//bring his lips [mm.]'s within distance of the opening = just so she could feel his static and breath.

-Oi yoi-

Quex and Yody and Flücky showed up and shoved the Chugger over off to the edge of the table. They huddled around each other/separated by the pitcher. The waitress came by quick to ask them if they needed any glasses = they serve guys like Dumbdumz/big Moonstomperz because of thy're hammerheartz = inside is outside = you talking to me.

-3 more mugs for my brothers here and another pitcher-

-Why not just get 2 pitchers-

She smiles. She's pretty volk.

-Sure and 4 shots; jimmy beam-

Quex was taken back by the girlie;

-That waitress, right, her name's Jane. I went out with her sister once. I had this weird wknd in Vermont with her and her family-

He waved his fists infront of his face like he was trying to stop someone from repeatedly stabbing him.

-…Her aunt has Alzheimer's and they let her go for walks//**A L O N E .** She'd been gone for 2 hrs. So we all go out looking for her. The police are with dogs and we're walking along shouting out her name…-

Quex cups his hands over his mouth like a megaphone:

-…EDITH…EDITH…So we're walking down this dirt road at night, looking and looking and we hear barking. It's getting closer all the time. So we turn around and see them behind us-

He's silent:

-…they were following **us.** The dogs and the police were following **us**-

The chug roles his saucer eyes and says:

-Thy're are alot of pretty girls here-

-Oi…-

(this is Vodden)

-…they don't breed mongrel scum either-

Vodden had a friend who was at Oka, right. Vodden kept the photo of the showdown on the wall of his and Nalene's flat.

He wasn't even looking at the chug when he said that—just looked at the kinderwhore.

Quex poured all his mates another round and skipped the chug but said:

-Come go with us-

(this is Vodden again):

-Yeah, come go-

-W'erewe goin-

-We'll finish and go somewhere else, meet the Reverend-

Flücky leans forward and looks round the table and sites Vodden's now empty mug:

-Yeah, I feel like bailing-

✖ ✖ ✖

They piled the indian in back of the pickup with Flücky. The rest got in the cab with Quex. The chug was like a dawg on a big trip to town.

Flücky pulled out a flask of firering liquid.

-Here, you want a swig-

The indian was enchanted. He reached for the flask.

-Nah, nah, nah, Pastor Scott and Rev. Butla, remember? No touch you just open up and I'll pour. THIS I COMMAND-

The Turkey ran down the sides of the chugs mouth cauze of the movement of the truck. Flücky was pretty good at aiming. He'd done it enough in deuces before. The day he showed up for an exercise straight, would the be day he realized where the enemy was. Right now/he was just numbout/aim and shoot...

✖ ✖ ✖

-We finally find her up to the waist in snow; screaming her head off-

Yody muttered something about Ian Stuart and Flücky looked confused.

-He pulled a Jayne Mansfield, didn't he-

-But the snow fell-

-phukyou...-

Jane brought another pitcher. Quex paid and Flücky proceeded to hit him in the back.

-I'll play mother-

Yody held out his glass.

-The beer in europe is better-

-You've been to europe/you fuk-

-I get great postings-

Flücky says;

-They do. I hear-

-Where the fuk you been in your career Flücky-

-Aid to the first power: busting up protesters-

Quex nodded in agreement.

The beer glugged up in the mugs. Secret/if not patronizing: Yody's smile/it was. He had been everywhere. Flücky put the pitcher down and pulled out a pack of cigarettes. He offered one to Yody then to an empty seat, that no one was there no more, and Quex showed his fangs. The seat could've had one as well...not no more.

-Oh, sorry, here have 2-

...and he proceeded to talk to the chair about a movie he had seen. Yody infos Flücky that the chair was probably less responsive because it hadn't seen the movie.

-It might be able to drink-

-Good, then let's cooperate-

They all raise there glasses in a toast as Vodden stares off at the kinderwhore. She's sitting with some new people. I think the platinum shorthair vagen is her limpdick boyfriend. She gets up and gets lost in the crowd with him.

-How long were you posted there-

-A year, shnook...didn't you miss me-

-No...no-

-Quex-

The voice came from G-d.

-How are you-

He had arrived at the table without Quex noticing. G-d was very tall and looked alot younger than most of the Dumbdumz. He waz snorky. He always had a bowler, tailored crombie or sharkskin or a harry or some shit like that. They used to use hiz grommet mug to card him, just cauze/to hold off on too many baldheadz in a joint.

-Flücky, Yody, Vodden, how are you-

-hey...-

Killer Pepé wazn't inthuzed...he didn't favor the

crew none too much...but he tagged because he waz seeing G-d. He waz rude—in more wayz than one—to them kind. But he inspired dread. Killer Pepé waz a wicked sonofabitch. He got hiz name from a Edward G, Robinson movie—Lil' Caesar. He packed a ratchet. Killer waz rhygin. It waz de butt he kick = I Edison saw him give da boot to 2 visiting NF types and, I don't know what he waz—some bad minded backwoods mutherfuk, that bought a pair of DMs and thot he waz down wid it, BY HIMSELF.

Killer pulled a Pollock on the guy's face—crazy ratchet pallet knife and aggro body twistin. I mean, Killer waz bruised for the wear—lost most hiz vision in one eye, but he won and got pack of smokes out of it too. 'Cauze they fell out one the boneheadz' jackets when they fukkin ran, man. He waz or could be— **PURE FUKKIN EVIL.**

They weren't too inthuzed to see Killer, either—so you got a deadlock.

G-d grabbed a pint and took the empty chair. G-d asked;

-No one was sitting here/right-

Killer waz off to find hiz own seat.

✖ ✖ ✖

So he met him...

*You should haf seen hem he waz a beauty/areal lil'- darlin in blk stingy brim, new harry and a snorky pair of* old oxbloods. He's maybe jus a lil over me n I'm not too tall myself. He waz ras.

I got to see him mostly at this pub house on thursdays. He jus sits by himself n readz n drinks til his crew shows up—a book, hez got always spread eagle, pulled apart by booth of hiz wide finger tipped handz. Hiz face pulled into it. I wont to go over n talk to him, alot, but I never got the noive.

I'd knew I'd treat him nice though. I see him alot walking around. He waz rude for sure. He had the wickedest crew. 'Thy're boss a'yite breddaz', I guess,' he'd put it. But I could bust a nut over him iz wot I say. I alwayz could for Sparker.

It waz amazing. Why doez he look at me like that, real sweet, wid thouz big blk eyez n that smoik.

I saw him the other day wid that gutter Skin, Eddy, sittin ontop of a newsbox on the street. Jus starin down at me. He's too rude. He's too stackt—what a neck, such a smile. He's got lips, up close, that could stop a speeding train. So soft, I could use my mouth n finger to meet it and leave my fist to hold my heart.

It's fun to see all of it go down. It waz, whatelse could happened wid thoze 2—wot goez on inside…

Sometimez like last week, I look over n he's jus look'n at me. He noddeds n I cant go over or say some'n. I figured it would be stoopid, the thingz I would say—and the boneheadz bugz me hiz wid. I don't think my crew would *not be thrilled wid these gooberz—no fukkin way, mister. He couldn't even come over and say hi wottup. How long could I keep readin that fukkin book. I need to get a res somtime n that would be jus look'n o'er to him. He waz caught, somtimez, starin back, but he don't come over or say hi...nah no, that don't cop shit, bredda. I n'er made a move beside an eyeball mov'n over hiz direction once n'while. Then I get my face back btwn the pages. Somtimes I'm jus star'n at the woidz n his face appears n I kiss it. Hiz lips r wide n soft. I figure he'd turn hiz hed roun n smile 'cause he's cute like that, I figure. But I'd still have hiz neck to breath against n hear myself escape from his mouth. Iz he goin with that bonehead?*

Strange though, it all happened to Killer lookin for a chair one day:

Speak to me...

-Yush, anyone sitting here, buddy-

-Nah, nah, ga hed-

-Nice stingy...-

-You never seen one before-

-Don't be crass-

-It's my middle name-

-Kiss me neck, yush, you are a smartass, aren't ya-

-Ruffy, Horde, sameting, if you're asking dumb questions-

-Like you guyz keep a low profile. I'm not fukkin impressed. Anyone sitting here? guess not, yush-

Killer went to grab the seat and walk.

-What do ya think-

Sparker shows him the lining of his harry,

-I just got it to replace my flt. It's boss 'rite? They were never slaves-

-You're not a stewart-

-I'm not a slave-

-They owned them-

-Before you head on back to Babylon: I'm Sparker...don't be a jackass—mek a fren tadeh-

I remember when Sparker took hiz hand. He shook it. One hand (softy) held Killer'z n thother reached over n touched the top, enclosing the whole thing. Sparker jackt hiz head back. He started to chat him up n stuff. Pretty obvious, Killer'z an attractive guy—in puggugly sort of way.

I Edison figure he liked him then. Guybye wazn wot Killer waz sayin....

G-d frowned.

**✖ ✖ ✖**

Check ça, man, this boss shit doesn't happen alot. It'z goin to be a cool night. There'z a great band playing, whose music iz sweet, thy're there to pump the hoolibwoyz/all the Rudies—the Finger Mashers a name straight from Lee "Scratch" Perry. I like Joe Gibbs and Sparker'z at the tablez. You don't get to hear this shit usually: true bashment tunes. He just cranks the shit. Nobody stays down—except for Yody. Quex iz usually right in the middle of things stomping having a blast—which iz rare—seeing *him* smile. They shuffle like the Moonstomperz did in JA, way back in '64 and stuff before that and after and now. I can be there too when I hear the beat. There's no upsetting it, except for one. I dance slow to upset the aggro pace in babylon. I don't dance out of frustration. I don't march in one place. I Edison move slower like the hooliganz did with ratchets strapped to their bodiez, hidden away like little vandalz. Dem, they conquer the beat, the floor, the dancehall.

Whatz ˢᵒᵒᵖⁱʳcool: The Horde are here. Thy're Sparker'z crew. Thy're Ruff Riders, the snorkiest bandits—even more than the Dumbdumz. You got Mark and then Re:Mark—thy're are 2 baldiez called Mark so...go figure, Bomb, Cyco, Kreeg, Zombie (he'z the drummer for the Finger Mashers—you got to talk to this dude if you wont to find out why he'z called Zombie), and Roadkill—they found him outside a Subway Thugs/Templars show passed out, spread, ready on his back, on the street. He waz pissed to high heaven. He kept mumbling something like 'you can't trow me out.' They just watched for awhile deciding what to do, laughing, asking him if he wonted a beer, seeing if a truck wouldn't swerve in time...adoption waz the only option. Turns out he came from Port Alberni via Virginia—so they were doing him a favor by telling him he could hang wid them and not go back. Canadian Gothic may appear to be less interesting than American, English, or German, but it is equally as bizaar. Him like me, I Edison, a bastard American landing in Viccoma Head, County. A entire ground that had sold itself out, to become a degenerated ditto copy, of the heartless freakshow of Hollywood Blvd., or maybe, the glam nightmare of South Central, or perhaps, sometimes, to dream of the televised civility of a middle-class English tea party. Him like me, a fukkin expatriate, declaring a hell whole lot of territory—the road waz hiz start. I got the corner with my stand—*c'est* too *bon*.

They grabbed the table where Sparker waz sitting. I Edison got up, went over, and gave greeting. Sparker got up,

    -Hey, Eddy, got to start now. ...get a new jacket
    there, Eddy, why don't-

and went to get the tunes going. I Edison got his old one. He ditched it one night. It's burnt in front but I keep it clean and it woiks. Sparker, he was never a nigga at anything. You could tell by the way he dresses and walks—he'z always been Blk. He taught me all of that too. I Edison, I've never been, too. I don't know—he'z jus too ras.

    -Eddy, how'z our bredda? grab a seat. Let us get
    you a beer-

and these guyz know how to get to your heart.

Ah yes, the Horde on one side Dumbdumz on the other. You got to hand it sometimez for urban renewal. Wot can I say?

-Yeah so you don't like girlz-

I Edison thot they were laying in to me again, but nah, it waz all copacetic. It waz something to do wid Zombie.

-Nah, nah, nah, I didn't say that. I said, that putting that goil in Jonny Quest waz a stupid idea. Jonny Quest iz a guy show and goilz don't fit. Just look what they did to Hadji…-

Cyco askes him,

-Wot did they do to Hadji? he's bigger that's all-

-Nah, he's not fukkin bigger. He's…-

-He went through puberty-

-I don't want to talk about that-

-Puberty-

-This iz Jonny Quest-

-He's a cartoon-

-Yeah-

-Who went through puberty…-

-Nah…-

-…wid Hadji-

-Hey, look, Hadji iz a computer geek now and the goil, she's fukkin annoying-

-That's Race's lil girl-

-Yeah, ok, how did Race get a kid-

-You don't know this Zombie-

-You're talking about sex again and this iz Jonny Quest-

-Did you ever think…like the idea came across your mind maybe, that Race Bannon waz having it off with Doc Quest-

-No! and I read a book about that stuff and homos can't breed-

I wazn't going to say something to that cauze it came from Zombie. But Re:Mark said something about turkey basters?

**✖ ✖ ✖**

You know, I love dancing. I'm having such a bon temp. I'm pissed and I'm ripping shit up. And you know wotz, wotz? wotz better? when I'm wid the crew, things are copacetic—I Edison feel safer. I feel good. I Edison don't feel like some aggro bAKRA backwoodz motherfuk looking for a fight iz going to noize me up. Mostly, the monkeyz do it cauze they figure they could take me—especially if thy're not alone—like az if monkeyz do anything alone. But I digress. I'm having fun, rite, and all iz well.

Ah, fun a dying art. People think you need drugz to have fun. No. You need beer. You need drugz to have sex.

One moment and everything fallz into place. The joints hollering to the Mashers and making a noize—it all doezn't matter now.

Me, Killer, and the the Horde all got askt to Sparker'z family'z place for the 4th Bar B'Q. All I could say iz;

-Any pork-

-No...no-

-...ah , gud-

**✖ ✖ ✖**

Sparker'z mad cute n freaky. He let me crash on his couch that night. Sparker'z not ascared of me. He'z not ascared of nothin/nah/not him.

-Eddy, I took you out of all that shit, and w/out the grief, didn I-

-Wha-

Ah, he'z getting on that stuff that he did for me when I Edison first got to the beach. My family and stuff.

-...getting out of yer family's business-

-Wha-

-Are you still in business-

-No,not no more, no-

Wow, he could stare a bredda down, I tell ya. Sparker'z got beautiful eyez.

-Did you jack a car to get that seat, Eddy-

-You could get a seat in any junkyard-

-Pretty new seat, Eddy-

-What did you hear, Sparker-

-Nothin no more, Eddy-

-I could still be a bootblack-

-If that's all, yeah-

-Great-

-You talk to your family lately, Eddy-

-No-

-Good. Lose Bragger, Eddy-

It waz a good fukkin day, all day.

He likes Pepé. He loves me. I Edison know. Most people, especially bAKRAZ, find out that thy're fukt or whatever and they start to strut down the runway like thy've been condemned or sometin: dementia dry humpin in syncro. They got this look like they smellin somethin allathe time—total stad scene. fuk that. Take me for what I am, huh.

✖ ✖ ✖

Things feel cool on the porcelain. Prochain ran his finger down the side of Elie's head;

-All that belongs to me-

-I got to go find a place. I think-

Prochain goes off to get some juice.

## Instant Noodles and da Spanish Bwoys

…some people just have more to worry about…

There wazn't much open past 2 a.m. Prochain had to walk past pigeon park where the scaghead whores and the dickless nod boyz parked themselve forever/ever. Thiz garçoon startz crossing over the street to him. There waz a corner store run by gooks. They over priced shit but you could pickup smokes/nuts/milk and those noodles they got every welly case and workingclass volk addicted to = 4 for a fukking dollar/but not at this hr. Now/they get you a good = 35/65¢ and maybe you could get an egg too and something filling. No protein in that shit. But the chimps got to eat.

-Hey, you couldn't lend me six bucks could you-
Prochain kept walking.

-Are you going home? If you lend me sixbucks, I
could make it back by the end of the night-

-No man,I ain't got six bucks-

-I could make it back and give it back to you by the
end of the night-

Prochain stopped at the corner hoping the garçoon would keep walking. But the kid stops too/and pauses too/just lollygagging around.

-You want your boots shined Prochain-

-No. Eddy/whattup-

Yeah/yeah/Prochain chat it up with me/only because you got that kid skankin you. I hear you still got that cutey. He's up in that rez. You keep him there donchay phukhead.

-Sameoldsameold-

The garçoon is still tagging. But he catches a wiff of a snailing car and walks toward it, nonchalantly, trying to be noticed.

-Hey/look/I'll see you around/OK/Eddy-

-Sure Pro-

You shorteyedpsychopeddyfuk.

✖ ✖ ✖

Yody couldn't feel his joint. He didn't feel this violent guy thing. He'd cum so sublimely/just a tingling feeling through his body. If Cathy hadn't been swallowing and the gummy glop wasn't on the sides of her mouth/he wouldn't have known. He was happy just the same.

# Hellbent

Yody and Cathy lived just below Prochain. The papermaché ceiling shot off scan modes of Prochain fukking around. Thy'd hear the bumping and yammering all on forever/because he wouldn't shuttup or rest. You should have heard him jacking, man, he just shouts Henry'z name so fukkin loud...it's just damn embarrassing man...like when he leaves the windows open—[woah].

-This is the part I like best-

Quex was sitting on the couch with the war flag framing his bulky middleweight frame. There was almost a glow 'round the shiny's clear smooth head: Die Strasse frei dem sturmabteilungsman.

-Odin's Law...-

-Shutup/listen/listen-

Yody got up off the couch and crawled over to the sound system. He cranked the volume up and tilted his head toward the speakers. Quex waited and listened for the powerchord burp.

-FUK/YEAH-

-THY'RE GOOD! BUT...ODIN'S LAW...//EVEN THE BRUISERS//FUKKIN OI, MAN-

-THAT'S NOT THE POINT... THAT'S NOT THE POINT! I DON'T KNOW; I STILL THINK THIS SHIT BOOTS//IT KICKS ASS—FUKKIN,

**BLASPHEMY, MAN!,**
SLAYER,
FUKKIN EMPEROR//
**BARD! YOU, FUKKIN ROCK MY WORLD, CAT!..-**
-...BARD, MAN, THAT DUDE'S CRAZY ASS//'I FELT LIKE IT'//*AMERICAN PSYCHO*, SHIT. HE SHOULD HAVE BEEN IN THE OLYMPICS WITH THAT EVENT, YODY//THEY EVER MAKE SOME TOURS IN THE SOUTH A FEW YEARS BACK? LIKE SUMTER. 'MEM-BER THOSE CHURCHES GOING DOWN LIKE RICE HOUSES.... EVIL, EVIL NORWAY-
-DAMN SURE, TRU DAT, BROTHER!
-NORWEGIAN PSYCHOS-
-IT'S A BIG WAKEY/WAKEY/BOY HOWDY! THEY'RE BORED AS FUK, LIKE ME AND YOU-
-NORTHWEST PSYCHOS-
-FROM ONE BARREN WASTELAND TO ANOTHER-
**-UND CANADA! ÜBER ALLES-**
-RIGHT! FROM ONE BARREN WASTELAND TO ANOTHER! BLASPHEMY KNOWS, BROTHER. THEY KNOW-
-BUT, YODY, YODY//THING IS...THE BAND-
-WE CALLED THEM. YOU KNOW WHAT WE CAN CALL UP, QUEX. YOU GOT A CALLING. YOU WERE DOING DINKY HALFASS SHIT FOR HELLIN HIPPIES ON HARLEYS AND THEN **bLAM!** YOU'RE ON YOUR OWN. YOU CALL THE SHOTS...-
-... I KNOW THAT "DAMIEN" CAME OUT OF SOME-

WHERE//...//I GOT SOME BUSINESS WITH FAG-GOT//...//I GOT TO GO FIGURE...-

-YEAH//...//OK-

-IT'S JUST T.C.B—HARD WORK...-

-//...//CHALICE BEARER! FUK OI! FUK OI! FUK ALL OI!-

-FUK OI? HEY, THAT'S PRETTY HARSH, YODY-

-THIS IS A WICKED PART. DID YOU SEE THE VIDEO I GOT OF THEM-

-...AND YOU KNOW WHO'S IN THE BAND/FUK OI?-

-WAIT FOR IT WAIT FOR IT WAIT FOR IT//...LISTEN//...//FUK YEAH-

-YODY, YOUR SHUTTING OUT, BROTHER? IT WAS MURPHY'S LAW, BRUISERS AND WARZONE... MAYBE, A LITTLE SKA...-

-FUK SKA, QUEX-

-OH, MAN, BROTHER, I SAW YOU TOE TAPPIN TO THAT TAPE THAT SPARKER LEFT AT THE SHOP...-

-"MY GIRL"//ONLY MADNESS-

-THAT'S SKA-

-NO IT'S NOT-

-COMEON, YODY-

-YEAH, WELL, YOU KNOW, QUEX//"THAT WAS '69. THIS IS THE SPIRIT OF 88.' AND...-

-...PUMPIN FUK TO EVERY FRIGGIN GLOSSY ISSUE OF RESISTANCE = HANGING ON BURDI AND LONG'S EVERY FRIGGIN WORD. TATTIN TWINKIES...

-WHAT...-

-...BEATIN DOWN PAKICABDRIVERS. FRIGGIN,

CHRISTIE, ZUNDEL…FRIGGIN, KIN OF MILITIA BOMBERS SITTING AT MY COFFEE TABLE. FRIGGIN, PEOPLE COMING IN AND OUT OF THIS SHITHOLE TOWN, I DON'T EVEN WANNA KNOW…-

-THAT'S…-

-…AND THEN IT'S, "FUK OI!" AND ALL OF THIS GREAT DAMNATION! HEILE! DARK DAEMONS FROM THE DEPTHS OF THE NEVER…FRIGGIN THINGYZ AND UNNAMABLE WATER DWELLY UNKNOWABLES BORN OF…-

Yody's guests had to be tored apart by his sonic arsenal…. He'd debate over the cookie monster music, the Oi the R.A.C… It was going/realbig/especially, now = Yody got a new player/with megabass. So now he could hear the double floorbass/heartattack/muchbetter—good.

-YOU COULD TAKE ALL THAT **SKA** AND **OI!** SHIT, BUDDY—TOSS IT. JUST PUT IT AWAY. GET RID OF IT. LET IT MOLD. IT JUST DON'T MOVE ME, MAN. IT'S CANDY ASS; WITH THE HALFASS TINNY GUITARS AND BULLSHIT BITCHIN ABOUT SWEET MOTHER-FUKKIN ALL AND THE PUB AND THE FUKKIN 'ME N'MY FAGGASS, LIL'BITCHES'//"YAH, MON". I JUST DON'T GET THE FUKKIN AGGRO—**'PICKITUP·PICKITUPPICKITUP'**—DAMN THAT SHIT TO HELL, BROTHER. JUST GIVE ME, RIGHT NUFF, PISSEDOFFTITUDE, S'ALL. WHO THE FUK CARES ABOUT A 'FIGHT' AND 'SATURDAY NIGHT.' THIS IS THE PACIFIC NORTHWEST! NOT SOME COCONUT

THROWIN MONARCHY PANTYWAISTLAND//WE'VE HAD BLACKS, CHUGS, CHINKS, AND TELEVISION FOR YEARS, HERE//24/7//LET THEM FUKKIN DEAL WITH THAT!

I WAZ A KID, HERE. I WAZ TEENAGER, HERE. I'M STILL FUKKIN, HERE, BROTHER. I JOINED THE FUKKIN ARMY, MAN—METAL MILITIA, KISS ARMY, GUN AND KHAKI REALMAN'S ARMY—WHATRYWE-GONNADO, NOW, SGT? 'I WANT WORLD FUKKIN DOMINATION!' YES, FUKKIN, SIR!

I KNOW ABOUT TACTICS. I WAZ TAUGHT STRAT-EGY. I KNOW ABOUT GUNS, I KNOW ABOUT ASSAULT WEAPONS, I KNOW ABOUT THE FUKKIN SITUATION. I KNOW ABOUT THE FUKKIN MISSION. I WANT THE G-DDAMN EXECUTION! IT'S MY FIST, MY GUN AND MY FUKKIN HEAD, WHICH IS TOTALLY FUKT WITH BUT NOT FUKT AND I'M PROUD OF THAT!

I NEED SOME REAL SHIT, THAT'S GONNA THUN-DER THAT, BROTHER!

and Yody gets into Quex's face for this one;

CHECK THIS OUT, BROTHER! CHECK THIS OUT!

# BLAAAASPHEMYYYYYYY!!!!!!...

What Quex wonted to feel like saying waz 'YOU ROCK! I'm there witchu, brother, in some sorta ways.' But being with being the way he is, and has been, lately, what came out waz this pause—a long, double long, pause:

-//...//...//**IT ROCKS**/IT SHREDS/IT GRINDS/IT'S COOL...//...//BLAH. BLAH. BLAH-

Yody got off, big time, on metal and white noize. He'd figured, Ol' priests had thunkt out the mojo, along with the soundtrack, in groovey paperbacks, ages ago. Some people, they figured that one thing didn't fit from the one to the other. Like, he didn't have any hair to whirl 'round or nothing. It waz simple shit to go figure...

Yody's waz...him with Vodden, they'd been trying to call and conjure—rings and metals and silks//thingyz and juju. Vodden and Zombie then Faggot and Vodden, they waz calling up G-d, nightly. They waz watching videos with G-d/thinking shit up/and now and then/as it waz/then/with Quex on the rollcall, as well.

The Dumbdumz had riddin into magnificent infamy. They'd gearedup in blk//had an inner circle of heavy duty thuglife combat cowboy showdowns, going pretty ruggid. The Dumbdumz, they found the signs that waz right and woiked//crashing parties, tearing shit up—shrubs and ravers, wellyboyz, gutterpunks and dealers—sometimes heading out to the hoovervilles over on the otherside and disturb them and what they don't got. It went way far from Blasphemy groupy'n. It waz Dumbdum and them//the ol'boiz to high priesten thugz/feeding holocaust barcodes to big'ol thingyz hidden behind rockpiles and barwired campsites//they waz calling up thunder—

something like comicbook crossover/trade paper-
back//Chuthulu meets the W.C.O.T.C.

-ODIN'S LAW...THAT'S LIKE WHAT, QUEX? WHAT?
YOU LIKE THE ANTI-HEROES AND RAHOWA, TOO,
STILL-

-...THY'RE COOL—NOT NO MORE, BUT THEY'RE
NOT NO WAY NEAR LIKE ODIN'S LAW, OR
BLASPHEMY-

-YOU LIKE BLASPHEMY-

-YEAH, I LIKE BLASPHEMY. I SAID THAT, YODY-

-THEY ROCK-

-THY'RE TRUE-

-CHEERS-

-CHEERS//...//YOU GOT ANY FEAR-

-//...//LEE VING WAZN'T SERIOUS//YOU KNOW
THAT DONCHA, QUEX-

-//...//I FAVOR THE TEMPLARS AND THE UPSET-
TERS, NOW-

-THERE'S A JUMP...-

-BETTY EVERETT...-

-WHO...-

-...I LIKE THE "SHOOP SHOOP SONG", YODY-

-SHE SOME PUNK CHICK-

-...FISHBONE...PASS ME A BEER, THERE, YODY-

...but there was none left;

-HEY, CATHY/CAN I HAVE BEER IN HERE?
QUEX, IT'S FUKKIN INSANE WHEN THIS SHIT
COMES TO TOWN. G-D'S A FOLLOWER, OF THE
REVEREND AND PASTOR, TOO-

-KILLER AND G-D...I/I/I DON'T WANT TO TALK ABOUT THAT SHIT, RIGHT NOW....-

-WHY NOT!? = FAGGOT'S, OK? BUT NOT G-D- -//...//-

-HEY/QUEX, I'LL MAKE YOU A TAPE-

-I'LL BUY IT = PIRACIES A CRIME-

**-SWEETHEART, COULD YOU GET QUEX A ANOTHER BEER-**

-...GEORGE NO MEK NO DUNZA THAT WAY-

-WHAT?...HEY DID YOU READ THAT ARTICLE? DO YOU KNOW WHAT THE FUK'S HE TALKING ABOUT-

-I HAVEN'T THE SLIGHTEST IDEA. I THINKS IT'S SORT OF THIS FUKT UP NIETZSCHE/RUSHTON THING-

-DID YOU EVER READ ANY NIETZSCHE-

-I FLIPPED THROUGH SOMETHING AT THE LIBRARY ONCE-

-...AND-

-I DON'T KNOW-

-MAYBE, IT'S BETTER IN GERMAN-

-YEAH, BUT WHO SPEAKS GERMAN-

Cathy walked into the livingroom with case of beer and dumped the brews infront of the coffee table. She turned down the volume and grabbed a bottle and popped it open/took back a gulp...

-Germans. Doesn't this make it easier-

-It's going to get warm sweetheart-

-Drink faster-

-...lets get Flücky, Vodden, and G-d over here-

Cathy spat out a gob of beer and wiped the stuff what drooled from her bottom lip. This kind of reminded Yody of something fun btwn them the night before. But she...

-You're not bringing those fuks overhere...are you? I can't deal with Flücky tonight. I'll belt him-

-It wouldn't be the first time, so whats the problem-

-No. Call. Goout/go out and solve a govt conspiracy theory...go abuse forners; but no idiots...-

**-Dumbdumz-**

-Monkeyz...whatever!...not here, not tonight/OK/ I've been working all day and you're already getting on my fukkin nerves, **D A R L I N G** -

-Like what? you have guests comin'-

...and she flopped down onto an easy chair and put her bootz up on the coffee table.

-You know Yody, you're a little bitch-

-Me? I'm a lil' bitch? I'm no lil' bitch. Why'd you call me that? I'm no lil' bitch, sweetheart. Me and my bro, we jus be kickin'/tro'n back a few...-

-Yeah-

-Right. No problems. ...loosen your girdle, sister, stay awhile-

-Yeah, Yody-

-//...//Yeah, what-

-I got company coming-

-Who-

-Why-

-I want to know-

-Why-

-Cause-

-Cause what-

-Wha...-

-I don't have to tell you who's coming over, Yody-

-Wel...-

-I don't have to tell you jack. You know like, who the fuk are you...-

-Not a lil' bitch//...//-

-Silvie and Gina-

-Naaaaah, you go on witchor badself-

-Piss off-

-//...//-

-We went to school together. There's no problem with that. ...and something happened-

-What-

-Why, Yody? why don't you go about your business-

-Isn't Zombie seeing Silvie, now? I see them keeping company—there's something in his blood for that. You talk about Blasphemy, Quex, check this out, huh, Zombie, huh-

-Wow,...from a small town, HUH-

-What the fuk is up with...-

Quex, sayz, cauze he'z just getting more tired and angry, and protective;

-I'm getting tired of all this shit, anyways, Yody. I wanna bail, man-

Quex hitched up his braces, grabbed Yody, hiz don-

key jacket and dragged their sorry asses out the door.
Yody loved Cathy.
So did Quex...

✖ ✖ ✖

Elie was in the corner slumped in a chair with his legspread. He was scanning the room, his head shifting from one flat cracked panel to the shotgun in the closet. The bass had stopped from down below. The shouting over the bass had stopped from down below.

Prochain walked in and out of the bathroom preparing drinks for them. He kept some scotch in the medicine cabinet along with downers, rubbing alcohol, rubber gloves, and cyclocort for his crackedhands. Prochain made a circuit btwn the bog and the little desk he had next to his bed.

He was popping spedderz and fiddlin with his inch wide braces. His eyes was all woren. He thot of police weeping. It was warm here and he could smell the alcohol on his own breath. If that was the case/in the morning it would be all over his new clothes in chunks and goo.

A hand tugged at his nipple.

-Get comfortable. Like I said you could crash here for as long as you want-

All teeth he saw

[thy'D bLOW tHEIR mINDS oUT tOGETHER]

and a maga bone ripped chest.

-You had a bad last few nights/chimp/just relax a bit...everythings going to be good-

There waz murderz in the area and people defenestrate television sets...

-This place is fukt chimp/people just do things here....like thy'll throw television sets out the window/for nothing/no reason/like thy're crazy.

People are cold/friendly here/you got to get past that/then they figure what you're into and then they become tight. Really intense like tight/but you won't know who's who until you get into that group/and then all these secrets comeout-

Elie could smell the sound of the burning cigarette in Prochain's hand.

-Do you want to see him...-

Prochain went to his little table and pulled a Polaroid out of the secret drawer//inside there was the pile of Holohoaxer photos, Leonardo, and Duppy-

-That was him/he was so confused about things. I felt so sorry for him-

He passed Elie a glass of vodka.

-Which first-

There are those legs of Elie crossing the room to the desk. He takes the drinks and glugs it down. Elie starts to cough it back up. Prochain gives him a slap across the head.

-I'm glad you're here/just don't laugh/alright-

It sounded muffled with the mouth against the back of hiz hand.

-You know/that Duppy and stuff/all that phuktup-
shithole persons they are/you should stayaway...
Well, you got a choice//ha-
-I wish you wouldn't call me chimp-
-Why-

## Big up

Momz, Popz, Brothaz, Sistaz, Auntiez and Volk—hiz crews there. Everybodiez turned out tuff Top Skins, ruff, well sharp, Bandalous all—Sparker'z crew, not hiz family. A Volkishe gather'n. It waz a family wid transplanted southern roots: Afro-Am Southern Aristocracy—could trace their tree of life past slavery n I think to the 1st guy who built a hut—n everyone wontz to know 'bout me n Killer.

They talk...

They talk....

I Edison nod'z n chew'z labba labba—blah—bring come—too much!

Sparker'z bradder, Malik, got up on the picnic table n threw hiz plate aside n pointed at Killer n me n holler'd:

### ·I AM MY BRADDER'S KEEPER·

Sparker sayz:

-Hey, great, he likes you-

Tonight, cauze of the 4th, I would think wrong, Sparker'z pretty fukkin dapper.

...and Killer, he'z in a huddle wid the Horde. He'z just in a mean coma and lookin' dis way...

*I stared at hiz bradder wid my gud eye—n they jus came*

*closer to hiz face n I saw Sparker in hiz face in hiz eyez n you could see it n all there eyez n faces. I don't got somthin like Sparker.*

Killer'z having a time trying to make sense of what Zombiez talking about. Zombie, for one—he lives a bit in regret for the *Sieg sieg* tat that he got on his neck, when he was 16, and the swastikas on his armz. He'z got "Rebel Flags" there too, but he'z never been to the South. He hangz out with more nonwhite people than a wigger could only wet dream about. He thinks *The Turner Diaries* is the best book he ever read. He got a compact edition of *Thus Spoke Zarathustra* and thought he waz macc'n.

Zombie used to ride a board, though, until he waz 16. But everyone picked on him. Then this guy came from out of town and whispered stuff in hiz and other boichailz (like Vodden'z) earz. Zombie showed up in school only few weeks later with his head shaved and that Sieg sieg on his neck. Zombie doesn't ride his board no more—Zombie stopt along time ago.

Zombie use to give beaucoup de temp and energy to the Aryan cauze. He still feels, once in awhile, Germany waz robbed. He gets that way, less so now. He'z proud of hiz German heritage and Nordic background. Actually, he'z English (and other darker stuff, maybe schmadda, is what'z said) and doezn't have a trace of German in him. But the RAHOWA Web site told him different. Mark (Re:Mark is what we call him, cauze of the two) he'z really from a Viking background, and can't stand any of thoze guyz. It didn't help matters much that he called the wife of this Wp monkey, 'a nazi cow'—the bAKRA broke a glass in Re:Mark'z face. Killer came over, on that famous day, and just about took that phukwit and hiz friends out. Killer wazn't about to be pushed around by no friggin monkey, by nobody, no way, no how.

G-d watched...

Zombie tried to read a book again, the otherday.
-It sayz, that people are homos because thy're weaker than normal people and so they weren't meant to reproduce-
-But, ah, there's artificial insemination-
-Yeah-
-...and a guy could get hard pump it up and pump it out into anything. Doesn't mean he favored it-
-OK-
-...and then there's turkey basters-
-Yeah, I think my sister did that-
Why wouldn't Malik like me. I'm I Edison. I'm cool.

Sparker n Killer, they were way off over on the otherside of the yard.
-Let's get out of here Sparker-
-Later, maybe...it's cool. All kinds of shit happening here-
It's all over—the soundz//of Delroy Wilson. He's

croonin' on/on topic/spot on, 'bout comin' from poor-
ness and wid no glam. He'z got himself and some
sweet, sweet music to charm wid. How couldn't any-
body melt when joe common, wid no dunza and sim-
plelife, comez over sportin a shufflin woid.

-After...-

-...-

-What'er you starin at-

-Come with-

Nobody matterz at this point, I guess. Nobody waz out
to skank nobodiez heart.

Then thy're gone.

Wid thoze 2...it'z all thrash.


*...oh killer, I could crash into thoze lips. You should get
out of my head, sweetness.*

*...but Sparker he's got that smile wid a gap btwn hiz
teeth, alla the light got caught wid hiz eyez...*

## Be Quick: The Duppy Conquering

Perhaps, if I wrapped my armz around myself/it could be me or Bragger. My face is too round to imagine good Duppy's face. Where my bradder had fangs and rabbit teeth/Bragger had a gap btwn them that made him the cats pajamas.

Pop never took the family out to dinner because he said white people liked to watch Black people eat. He waz not happy with white people. He never wonted to be around them. He only worked for them. He hated them. He feared them. We were stupid if he waz going to fail in teaching us to fear them. Keep the name. Bring no shame to the family name—if you did—you were safe. The house waz safe. He'd done good.

Mom waz a white jewess with a fascination for Roman Catholic icons. She barely parléd a woid of anglaiz before she met my daddy. She waz schooled by nuns and wonted to be one but decided to marry my pop instead. A person can only stand so much gloom. We were off to a good start.

They waz sitting watching the Mills Brothas perform on a variety show. My bradder Duppy sat in the easy chair—dedicated. The otha day, he said I Edison screamed like a gurl. We all sat watchin a movie about killer berds—ripping people to shreds—gurls that looked like my best teacher and ones that looked like the ones in school. Then just in the afternoon when I came back from there I waz in our room in my brown cord overalls and this berd came in through the window and waz trying to kill me. Yeah, I screamed—a lot.

My bradder got disappeared a day after his own birthday. It waz a urban accident.

His body flying through the air like a trapeze artist in a circus.

Several object d'art firing from out a shotgun barrel across a room.

I hate circuses, because they got clowns.

I waz hiding behind a door from my bradder before he left. I don't know why.

Thy're like nightmares trying to make you laugh. (clowns)

Duppy asked where I waz/before leaving//said to Tim 'tell him I say 'bye'. Then **bLAM**//I Edison figured it waz a dry crack, like a Dolby button being pressed on it all. Ever since I could only picture holding him in the tub because my bradder waz such a soft hooligan.

Pop on the edge of the couch, mom waz on the other end—"Paper Doll."

She came in, she waz on the phone and she dropped it and she came in and grabbed me, the lil' bastard, she and pop had brought home.

I Edison waz never like my bradder. I never went to the schools he went. I never wonted to be like him. I never learned to speak with my bradder's locked jaw. I kept the drawl of my fathers and fore that. Why quit a brogue Rose? why quit me? lock me up in shame but my jaws are oiled and swing with a shameless beat.

I met a kid with a crooked heart when I waz 17. When I did, his name waz Bragger. He played organ. He waz religious. He didn't fear. He always stood straite. He waz taller than me.

*'Can you make a poem black and bid it to sing?'* This big bard like cullen reached out and stalled a beat.

I wonted to kiss him.

Duppy's frens waz marvelled to find out that I waz his bradder because I looked nothin like him. He looked more Italian, is what waz said, for the record. I didn't pass for anything but what I waz.

> I'm none too bright
> but I've got a bon coeur
> lots of heart
> like a boxer's jab
> a brilliant yob
> not like my bradder
> looking like Bragger
> but not in his arms.

2 years working Bragger at a bookstore, mostly because of his charming personality. He wasn't much of a *bücher,* but he could sale alot to the ofay on the big yanky holidays. It waz Bragger's smile...

I still wonted to kiss him.

They wonted his balls. I wonted him to wont my heart—starkus.

Thy'd watch—in fear of my Black body.


I watched "When hell freezes over I'll skate" it waz the first time I heard a langston hughes poem. Then I remembered
"...kill 'em"

He ran across the road to me—in his run: his legs criss crossing but not striking anything but the ground. His coat collapsing at his thighs, stretching his body from shoulder to toe. He opened a few top buttons of his donkey jacket and asked me,

-Hey, shugaboo! stick your hand in, ...reach-

I pulled a long stemmed rose out of his shirt pocket and the bud was taped to a card.

-I waz told not to give it. Guys don't give other guys roses but...it's yours dear'art-

The card waz hand drawn but what it said waz what name he called me w/ a cartoon heart in the centre.

Maybe, Bragger and me'd be da Wild Bunch. We'd wreck it up. Get in late/maybe/maybe/in the morning, I Edison might not shower/to keep the smell.

Just like that hughes poem I read "...kill 'em...".
I'll run wild wid the res [t].

I went out w/ Bragger to movies and then tripping lights. It waz him that said to go get some stuff.

-You got dunza still-

-I gots dunza and later we go…-

-Your place-

-…or somerelse-

So we trudged down out of the pub and found these bredda grommets who were standin on the corner lookin badass. It waz turning into a big day w/ Bragger.

-Where youz guys go after this-

-…around//why/you wont to come back-

The grommet w/ the hood froze at that comment and Bragger told him to chill/but the grommet couldn't/although/his girlfriend found it funny.

Bragger had a collie we smoked on the way back to the pub. I got excited and wonted to touch Bragger's hair. Bragger knew volk what could crank and walk

no shaking and nahno

clogging

straight up

he wouldn't let me come home. He waz affeared of me seeing the hoodiez and gallaryz/bloods not at their best. w/ I Edison there seein wotz wot—wot kiss could he ever get.

I done see no shame.

Shamefull tho how Duppy pass [es], [t].


We wonted to go catch the grommet back and make him another offer

but I felt bad as it waz

at his age

hangin
looking baggy
like a raggamuffin
thinkin hez fly
dammack
so
We walked on/went back to the pub.

If I were a lion—I could be tuff enuff for Bragger/who waz prettier than me and needed a giding flexing arm/which I showed off when I pored the pint down my throat and puffed on a cuban. I started thinking about the lady xxx next door from my squat. She said she'd give me a Christian baby

to

sacrifice to Satan. It's been in my head all day.

Bragger passed the pitcher to one side and leaned across the table to askx me if I wonted to go to the washroom.

-Hidy/hidy/ho Eddy…-
where you had to make it as an offering. (the baby)

[I am I am I…] animalxxx

I Edison looked at the back of Bragger's neck and wonted to run my finger down the spine.

hxxx…and saw a wire fence behind a store and concrete powder dirt. The xxx fence had to guard a HIGH VOLTAGE generator they were kicking the crap out of the guy xx…x (this guy) I edison thought I'd be next for going along w/ the guy in the store he said he had toys and other things xxxe my moms wazn't around because there waz grocery store connected to the toy place.

xxxI had said 'no' he asked me to come

    didn't say anything

I waz like those dumby people who can't talk.

T^he cement puffs of cloud were flying. No toys were around like the guy promised me. Nothing/not even something from my moms when they brought me back to her/nothing from her/not a word or sentence from her or my xxxx poppy.sayd nothing

    Braggerz mouth hit the back of my troat and I waz affraid to xxxxxx inhale too loud but I'd shuffle and shift and slap my fists into my front pocket after he tried to press up. Bragger had I Edison's hands in xx his pocket now.

    -Could you kiss me-

    I Edison's arms: you couldn't find anything there

    no choochoo trains

    ah nahno cranking sites

mostly, Bragger wonted to go downtown. But you couldn't find anything wrong w/ e my arms/only a messed up tat.... Bragger's tongue waz bitter/sweet

I Edison's

w/ the x stuff of his/I much aprrecix ated.it.

    He waz taller than me. He had soft lips like his fuzzhead//now I got to touch it now. Bragger fell back on the seat and almost cracked his back. Bragger waz turning over and my hands pushed down soft on his fuzz and got filled w/ a desire to push my lips on hiz neck.

xxx I Edison n Bragger hopped over the fence and ripped my hand on the barbedwire. We jumped down and found Bragger's store...

I sat down in a cushioned chair and sunk real low to make eyelevel w/ the xx books on the bottom shelves. There waz stuff inside them that peoplex liked. I could makeout some words from the stars that were lightbulbs.

w/ this cash from the till I could stay out longer and go catch back a grommet or see if Bragger waz still piss faced glazy eyed over me or still wonted me or watch girlies wid me or blow our brainsout downtown.

We climbed up over/hiding our faces from people. I put my hood up and tried to fight off a heart attack. I had taken a razor to xx my chest to dig it out/but you need a bone separator to get it to all. I could get a feel of sticky wet...and dubbed out thumping w/ all the treble gone.

AT STRIPCLUBS I SAW LOTS OF HOOCHY GIRLS. THEY DANCED AROUNDxxxxTUBES THAT CAME FROM THE STAGE...you could s-ck on my tube darling
                //but that waz behind the
fence//all bloodydirty dusty faced xxx (that guy)

-Oi, Eddy, come here-

It waz wet and my hood waz dripping. It fell infront and stuck to the sides of my face. It waz like the fuzz on Braggerx when I last toucht it. The rain could wash the piss off of I Edison's hands. Bragger smelled nicer than all the powdered and stale tuna that surrounded us back here in this place. My hood dripped all over his face. He said I waz 'phat as a blunt' and we were close to the dark and no one waz there. The rip on my hand gave me a tingle against his ribs. My heart kept moving so fast I waz getting bored w/ it. I took my eyes off the glint in his mouth//he waz like a pirate.

MYy bredda Bragger waz spread xxx eagled on ashvault and I Edison took his arms and wrapped them around me. His chest waz softer and mushyer, starkus. I remembered when I wonted to touch it. I Edison felt the shower on my back running btwn my rump and my legs. I couldn't smell anything, round him, nomore, but Bragger and the bitter taste of him at the back of my troat. I tried to catch a wiff and he rushed me up as I breathed heavy w/ my bredda/feeling Bragger's hair against my cheek/his dark ear in my face. A person can live with only so much gloom. I ran wild with a ragga slacker, fearin nothin in heart and hand.

## Fuk de Law

**...yeah, 'rite—me and Elie.** I Edison, officially, met him on this really hot day. So me and my slip away los-bwoy/Bragger—who by this point, iz really fukt up and hanging with fukkin hair dressers, are doing our job polishing jackass' docz and shoes. Well/he's not doing much, but watching/but I'm giving it my shot. This boichail, 'bout my age, and Prochain walk over. The kid had the same look in hiz eye'z that I Edison had when I first hit the beach. Prochain wontz his shoez shined. They were theze fukking suede shitz and you can't really do it. But there'z no talking to that loud mouth pushy bastard. Bragger just wontz to pound the crap out the pencil stick. Who doesn't wont to drop him—Quex, maybe. So I'm going 'like no, man, it can't do,' but he sayz//

-Look just brush some of the dust off. I do it all the time-

-So do it yourself, then-

-I want you to do it. You need money, right-

-But if I fuk it up you'll freak Prochain. You never mean what you say. You take it back 5 mins. after you say it and then it hitz you and everyone else in the face-

Because I Edison know, exscaghead or not//a junkie'zajunkie and they never live up to their responsibilities/especially with their shoez. He waz a retard before/even as a g.r.u.n.t..

-You just got to take me at face value and you won't-

What the fukz that suppoze to mean Prochain…and he startz blah/blah/blahing all over the place, while I keep checking on Bragger'z temper and littleman'z caking scabbedwristz. He doezn't do right by that kid.

But you learn that Elie just favorz dEVIL bulliez. I guess/he waz too fresh then. But you learn better that Prochain'z just one big fukt up headtrip like all the bAKRAZ.

-So comeon and start brushing-

-Yeah/yeah/OK. I'll do it; but don't freak when things go wrong-

I just take out a brush and scrub az much old polish bitz off it az I could and start to clean away. I mek more dunza at punk showz/thoze kids got cash. It getz expenzive being angry all the time so you need employment or bored parentz that vacation alot.

-So shugaboo, wotz your name-

-Elie…-

Then Bragger cutz in…

-Can I do anything for you Elie-

Bragger'z still doing thingz to his people that he shouldn't//just to mek dunza. I think even selling to bAKRAZ is still demeaning. I'd rather get checkedout by the enemy/rather than my own: how can you not take that personally? I did it, for awhile, but itz dummy, man. Mayzawell putout bullshit gangsta shit and have midclass bAKRA teens spend their parents' cash. Now that's Berry Gordyism inprogress.

-Later, I guess-

Prochain is more encouraging:

-Hey, no, babe you want something from him go ahead-

-A gram-

Elie doz a quick glance over to Pro, smiles and,

-2-

Prochain/the dumbphuk/reaches into his pocket and pulls out 2 X 50's and a mess of 20's and slippes it over to **me**. Actually he just dropz it on the beach and I Edison'm suppose to pick it up like a dawg. The crap ends up in the same place and it comes to rest in Elie's palm.

I sayz like;

-You know you sound like HR? ...here-

to Elie and give my Oxblood/Impact tape to him.

-I think you're cool. I wont you to have it-

...the whole truht—is like this...in the paper they said they found two carcasses in a shooting gallery apt building: two guyz in plastic bagz.

# Blud Clat

Quex waz good to Prochain all the time they were enlisted together. Prochain had gotten that deal that'd get him back for hiz kindness and courtesy. He made pretty allrite on it himself. He got to buy into hiz own tat parlour with Quex. But Pro waz around him more than ever.

Alicia hated him, real bad. She waz Quex's talkshow getolife girlfriend. When she got out of H.C., and all that crossovershit happened, she started to speak like a talkshownigger = allatshit. She could never talk right nomore. Alicia looked like she could hump hoodratz for the rest of her life. A backseat girl cabin stabbin away during drivebys. But actually, all she waz waz a dEVIL chick that gotoff on being called bitch and referring to Quex as a dawg. She made Prochain exist = he hated that.

She had a permed ponytail way on top of her head. Alicia tried to get an afro puff but//whatwasthatwhatwasthat/oh yeah = "Her hair wazn't AFROCENTRIC enough." So she got the puffed pony instead. Quex couldn't resist but to use it as a speedstick when she waz giving him bow. He looked into the mirror once and figured she looked like a huge Pez dispenser. He broke out laughing and she got pissed off at him for that. So, in order to cum OK, he doesn't look nomore.

Prochain didn't get off on her none too much. She waz into 'allat' and he couldn't take the gangsta bitch routine and he didn't unnerstand what she waz getting at most of the time she talked at him.

Alicia, she couldn't take hiz shirt.

He remembered over Quex's place she started in on him. Prochain had a thread of a line to cross before he went ballistic//he wonted to be a C.O.//he waz the guy, remember, who knew *1000 Ways to Die* by heart.

-So what does your shirt say-

-Part Animal Part Machine-

-Nice did you just get it-

-No This is 1 of the oldest things I own. I lost everything else through out my life. It really means alot to me...-

-Henry Rollins means alot to you-

-Yes he does. I...-

Quex formed like a teenage bear. He waz walking around with nothing on but a wifebeater and hiz boxers. He'd gone to get some beer out from the fridge. Highball waz tagging just at hiz side. He waz a cool dog—really tight with Quex—for over 7 yrs, now. He OD'd once. Pro left a batch of collie cookies out and it waz charcoal and water dishes for awhile. But he'z a cool now, sorta, pooch. Their bodies matched in hardness. Highball's mane was a match for Quex's mutton chops. Quex had tats across his armz—one clencht fist on hiz neck....

Prochain got distracted from what waz going

on/what waz being said/when he waz like that: like as if Quex didn't know. He started doing that to Prochain in the army. Eventually, he got everyone to call Prochain—Faggot—wid deep affection.

Quex gave everyone a fresh beer and said nary a woid. Him and Highball finally took a seat, on the couch.

-I waz just kidding Faggot you always wear that shirt. He's a computer salesman right-

Prochain shook his head like he waz trying to rattle that bracket around. His heart waz pumping/being so next to Quex.

Alicia sat back in her chair and took aim right at the words on Prochain's chest; then she stared him down.

-I like the No Means No version better. Did you ever see it Faggot? It's Really cool. It's got that sun thing on the back, but instead of that pissed off lion, it's like a happy face, and at the part at the top, where Henry has "Search and Destroy" thy've got something like...oh: 'Read more books.' But this part's really cool//because on the front, just like your's/it has, "All Human"-

Alicia just kept staring dead ahead into the crystal cold which waz getting dimmer and colder. Quex looked at the ceiling, occasionally sucking back a few sips of his beer.

-I don't fukkin care what the fuk No fukking Means No has as a shirt. I like this shirt and I'll wear it whenever the fuk I please. Henry is fukking amazing and you don't have to get into him. I don't care what your opinion is. You don't know anything about him. You've never seen him. You don't know what he's about. And I don't fukking want to talk about it. He's someone I respect and he gets into my head and I can get into his-

To which Alicia responded with:

-I bet-

Quex waz only trying to chill thingz out a bit when he suggested they finish up and go check out a movie.

-We'll go see *Chase* or *Johnny Mnenomic*-

-I've been good to you haven't I, Quex-

...Prochain had already gotten his inch thick braces in a twist. Pro got up and walked out.

-Fuk, Alicia, don't do that to Faggot, man-

-Wha...-

-Get out of here. I don't wont you around nomore, tonight-

Quex went to his room to get dressed. He waz so pissed off, he didn't even call her bitch to get her wet. He wonted to slap her like one, though, but he don't hit girliez, not even this one.

**-Getout, fuk-**

-Aaahhpack it up...//I mean, fuk—what the fuk is all dis shit? What da fuk iz dat-

# Love up

Quex woke up, early and prepared for work. Highball waz having a look out the window. Quex had to be there. He had a contract with these scooter bwoyz from seattle and other such Ruff stuff which make grand and gear mornings, past, now and will be days and events come to become what is said to be sooper horrorshow, of tattoos, touchups, and vendettas wanting to make good.

There are noises all over, no buzzing guns but talk. They come in directly into the little apartment room. Most things are separated and in his memory//cliquity/claquing**it misses with the point of living alone. Quex remains unaffected by the thuggish sounds. He hears a Bradley comic//big screech. He seez hiz Neat Stuff, Slim Harpo's biography—all perfectly pressed and sealed.

-Komme Highball. komme-

Quex filled Highball'z dish up with chow. He gave him good scratches behind the earz and Highball licked hiz neck.

He picks up a pot with an extra large handle and places it on the stove and takes pieces of chicken in his hands then places them down and goes to the fridge to get cheese. He places the cheese back and returns to the chicken, but now he's got to fill the pot with water. Buddy does Hate now…or should he fry it. There is no option—fried or roasted—it's only break-fast—too filling. If you take the skin off…this is repulsive**close the window. It is closed. If I don't get dressed, shower and dress, I'll be late but I got to eat. I'll have breakfast with fried eggs. This is reliable. Put the water out. He grabs a pan and places it on the stove, turns up the fire to a steady hissing blue, then leaves for his shower; only to return moments later to remove the pan from the flame.

A sudden machinegun splash then the sound of constant exhalation and Quex is under the water. He brushes the water away like dust. It continues to run over him, crawling over his feet and down the drain. Someone was once in here with him, a long time ago. What time is it?

He is dressing—slick trouzerz/white freddy/ braces/a snappy crombie//big and bouncy shoes/ looked smart**perfect plantation wear. Quex sayz goodbye to Highball. Dog doez daily morning 'miss you' whine.

Quex stops in the hall, clasps his hands over his head, turns to look back, then leaves, dragging his fists down the stairs; but stops at the bottom and returns to ensure that he has turned off the stove.

The train, it leaves at 07:10 hrs and it is O6:55 hrs. I'll have to run. No I'll get sweaty. They're not going to like me if I'm sweaty and smelly—not this early.

He walked and arrived late—the next train. He waz always in a rush, but always late.

The trees crawl by the window with no draft. Drafts usually indicate the speed**movement. There are small houses, bare land, signs and traffic, people running, dressing infront of their windows.

Facing him, in another seat, is a top Mod in a dark gray, 3 button hole tonic suit. He holds his umbrella between his legs//next to his left foot is a soft leather briefcase with a rose popping its head out from inside. I think he chose to fall in love today. Quex wouldn't mind that very much.

-I can't think of it-

A few people turned when he said that. Buddy with the umbrella and flower chuckled. Quex muttered some more and contemplated faking schizophrenia. The train came to a stop at the next station. It was raining—hard**somewhat, and thundering**slightly.

She could've been a flapper. Out the window, there waz a chelsea looking Quex's age, wearing a raincoat. She faced north and smoked a cigarette clenched between her lips—her handz stuffed in her pockets. Her short hair waz pressed down against her head**drip dropping pearls down her face. She's tall. It's more her legz than anything else. Her head never moves, only the longlegs, weighted, shuffling this way and the other//on occasion**on occasion//she'd remove her hand from her pocket and take another puff, then wedge the cigarette back between her lips//her hand falling back into place. She started to board.

My chest starts to feel funny. He looks out the window.

The wet girl flops down next to Quex. She brings her leg onto her knee. Water's dripping along her cheek and she wipes it away—sweet like.

-I donwanta meet these people-

-Meet who-

Quex would talk to her because maybe the train waz too loud and no one would hear them speak. Ah, something still tugging inside.

> -I am like a cracked pitcher//my soul my body//I hear a soft song across the train and a overheard hush. It's so doleful: it weeps straight through my chest. What's your name-

She laughed. This is good.

-Doris-

-Oh yeah-

The Muzak was turned up. A flip of the wrong switch, and someone had turned it too high. It was German and played note for note without intonation. All the parts meant to be sung or chanted were filled with a hollow flute, off key— still sounded sweet.

Things get dark, only a few electrical sparks inside the car then light again. He glances to his left. The chelsea is still with us, staring at him and smiling.

-I should get a watch that doesn't tick so loud-

-Meet who-

-I gotta go and do some work on these guyz-

-What kind of work-

-I do tattoos…got my own parlour-

On a bridge over to the city, marks of white pop and snap all over. The rocks and concrete poles separate water and patterns//like a work by a painter who Quex couldn't remember, because he didn't like art. What he did waz a skill. What time is it?

-Fuk-

-You got your own shop? What's it called-

-**PUSH,** ha-

-You're the new one that opened up-

-Yep, just about awhile ago/not long/no-

-I was thinking about getting something done, there-

-...dolphin on your ankle-

-No, a spider web across my left tit-

-//...//-

-Not too quick on the draw there...-

-I didn't know you had a mouth-

-What do they call you-

-I'm Quex-

-For real-

-Yeah-

-Bonehead background-

-//...//-

-Nevermind...-

-You like Betty Everett-

-Looking for a kiss, Quex-

There's still a rose sticking out of a briefcase. Quex waz certain that hiz face would have been camouflaged. Now buildings pass. The train stops. His clients would be waiting for him.

Quex leaves just behind Doris. They rose at the same time and faced each other. Doris smiled and stepped back. Quex walked down and out of the train, repeatedly tugging and adjusting hiz braces and coat. He waz going to meet the scooter bwoyz and all the bright muggs.

✖ ✖ ✖

It seemed Quex had to stay up that night. Hiz heart waz racing a like cardiacassault was going to hit. He and Alicia were pretending crack house home economics all day and making a joke about birthing a idiot baby and going on welly. This eventually led to alot of foreplay and Quex screwed up and looked in the mirror. So he had to boot her out, again.

He spent most of the early morning, horny and looking at the bacon and cheezeburger the waitress had brought him by accident and watching the ratz run from one corner of the diner to another.

Prochain walked in with Elie shuffling in behind. He told him to sit and introduced him.

-You know Elie-

-Yeah-

Quex, iz wondering wot Pro waz thinking?

-Elie, this is my friend Quex-

-Hi-

-What are you doing here-

-It's that fukking ponytail, man...-

Quex had this smile on his face—a very noivus inside type.

-...oh, shit/Look/look, check ça, right there-

-What-

-Phukkinratz, man. Thy've been doing this major construction and thy're just going crazy looking for a place to hide-

Elie sayz,

-I like ratz-

-Is that what bit you-

Elie touched the scab on his face and Quex's became clearer. Prochain told him it was a big one that did it, while Elie was sleeping.

Quex asks him,

-Was it a rat Elie-

-Yeah, a pretty/pretty rat/a nice one with no tits-

-A titless rat bit you-

-I had a dream: I fukt it first-

-You a yud-

-No-

-Why not-

-Huh-

-Nevermind, here, shugaboo, you want this cheeze-burger-

-Sure-

-I bet...kosher pork-

Without looking, Quex slid the dish over to Elie. He turned his attention back to Prochain.

-You know McDonald's is a total anti-Zionist conspiracy. Did I tell you that. Did you ever check their menus/and they have a bunch of Blks advertising for them/munching on these cheeze and fukking bacon-

-Shit, Blks don't eat bacon-

-Not to my knowledge, Faggot...-

-Niggers do-

Elie kept munching on the burger.

-What's a nigger? what's a Blk-

-It's good-

Elie was chewing so hard that it stretched the skin on his face so much it'd torn open the stitches//so he had this tear coming out his cheek.

Elie got amazed so easily, back then, like with all the other madcraziez, cutz n skinz. He saw them over shadowing the dumb dumb violence of the monkeyz in the schoolyard. Their honesty over their stance on spades only brought more attraction; like Duppy not giving a fuk or chatting him up like it was a dirty little thing.

Duppy had power in his woids. He believed and resisted all the bullcrap of himself not being bigger and better. He spoke tough/thug like—crunching fist woids//smashing bone to the back of a brain. His skin was a flag/pure and soft with soft fuzz/big hands//ruffian bruizer hooligan/postures of groovey authority.

-Here have a napkin. You got ketchup all over//Cute little monkey you got there Faggot. You've become a big bredda/getobwoy-

-Your bitch dresses like welfare coon. Oi, Quex, what do you do to get her off? paint your joint blk-

Quex smirked:

-I try to not look in the mirror and...-

Actually, Quex had **RAHOWA** tattooed across his abdomen, so she'd never forget the purity of his cock.

Elie, was wiping the blood off his cheek when he said;

-We can't speak in motion anymore. We have to sit to talk-

-I'm gonna get my gun and blow *your* fukking head off too-

-Faggot, now you're starting to speak like a hoodrat-

Quex lighted cig and said;

-Comeon-

He got up.

-Where we going-

-G-d'z-

-Elie's not finished his burger, yet-

-Fuk it. I feel like watching *The Tribute Video* and G-d'z got a copy-

-I thot you were sick of that shit-

-I'm sick of a lot of things Pro. Let's go-

They walked out into street past the scagheadz and shit. They had to get to a street where a cab would actually stop. Cities were places of dread, as far as Quex was concerned. But, Vodden lives, somewhat/way out/and look what the feds and shit do to him.

Quex wazn't quite quick on the draw, when it concerned what motived Vodden to stare at a snow filled television screen on his dayz off. But in a way/cities are kind of evil = Cain invented it.

# 3

**Push Up**

I went to see *Bugsy Malone,* when I waz little. It waz the first movie I ever went to see on my own. I had to take the subway and I remember what my bradder Duppy told me to do, the last time I waz on it//

-Feel it Eddy. We're going under water. Hold your breath-

I had read the book and bought the comic. Fat Sam's crew were too rude. *Velma*//I Edison waz totally inlove with her and she got to dance real slow in the movie. They described it real good in the book.

Not even that schnook, trying to masturbate next to me, could take my eyes off of *Velma.*

**✖ ✖ ✖**

G-d'z bent. It'z true = he went out with Killer Pepé and Killer Pepé gave him the air to see Sparker//the Dumbdumz call him coonskin = Ruff Rider type. They got p.r'z/nigz and otherz. Killer though, I Edison truely believe he'z inlove. Killer though, he waz never quite a Dumbdum = cauze he waz part wop and the rest fukt = he waz Moroccan/hiz daddy Muslim. I guess it waz just in hiz blood to be a walking contradiction.

G-dz spitting now, for losing Killer and, in a way, not finding himself a beauty like Sparker = kinder inside.

G-d had a big collection of videoz and magz and flagz. He could mail order with the best of them—never had a problem with customz. They only gave him a hard time with the battyboichail shit—they had file started on him for that. But he could get hiz Nat'l Alliance stuff good and any other racialist stuff. He'd just order some comix and this cool badge for hiz flight.

After catching the first act on the tribute video; Prochain decided that he wasn't going to see Elie no more—he wonted one of them on the screen. He'd seen one monkey siegheiling in the front row of the concert.

-I hope he really doesn't like that guy-

-...which-

-The lead singer that lookz inbred-

-Nah/Pro/don't worry/hiz armz not high enuff. He'z just doing it out of habit-

-I got a bigger bozak than him-

Prochain asked Quex and G-d if he could get hiz head shaved while Rahowa sang.

-Why don't you just wait for that show we're going to-

-Comeon, now, you been good, so far, Quex. I've been good. Got you money, when you needed-

-...yeah, très bon, Prochain-

-So get it done so's I can look good-

Az they put the clipperz to Prochain//Quex started looking at him with the same consideration Prochain had just offered Elie.

✖ ✖ ✖

So at Sparkerz place you just drop by. I Edison came by, like everyone doez, and seeing he wazn't there, hopped in, tru da window, flipped on some tunes from *For a Few $$$'s More* and took a res on his couch. He should be home soon.

Last week, he'z sitting down at the pub and he takes a swig of beer and looks out over all the crap stads in front of him and sayz;
-I hate this town-
-Well, yeah, you were born here- I say back.
-So you get it-
-How could I not-
-I just never wanted to admit it. I tried, though, all that patriotic shit, but this town sucks. I want out-
He'z been getting like that, lately. I Edison think it comes, partly, from being struck gaga over Killer. I think Killer wontz to see Blasphemy wid him. I think Sparker wontz to head off to see Justin Hinds and the Dominoes. And I also think it comes from working all day in a boiling kitchen when, the weather outside is 90 degrees in the shade. You just come out from hot to hotter. I'm sort of used to it, from DC and Georgia dayz and other parts that I waz raised. Sparker doesn't know what a dog day is.

Sitting there at the table are Silvie and Gina— thy're seeing Zombie and Mark. Mark's been keeping company with Gina for awhile...but Zombie, he met Silvie a little while ago when her roommate, this guy, this freshcut that came to town: a real doofus—no smokes, no cash, and all he could do waz dish out drunken grief. The coo'nard, he bailed on her one day, while she waz at woik. This puto split owing her rent. He left her 2 broken coffee cups and 1/2 a milk crate of hacked up tapes. He took all of the stuff Sparker made for her—It waz like this dis.

We all came over to see what's what and she, Silvie, who's one tuff chick (a shitholejudgeofcharacter, but one strong heart chick, all the same), finally, waz sitting there, on the couch, just sitting and thinking, after having all that schizo shit pulled on her, and she sayz one thing, looking up and around and she sayz, "Now, I'm scared."

Zombie, he buttoned the collar up on his harry, for her. He wonted to make her. He always liked her and hated that feeb for what he did—way before. She waz a regular Ronnie Bennett—a belle sex kitten. She got all the politesse. All us stayed and kept company and drank beer and sang stuff, we could remember.

The Ruffies went out on a ratpatrol. ...pulled their rubber soles up, just at the boarder, of where the stads come from, where he's from. They poored out some wicked juju around there. He don't come cross that line, no more.

Zombie, he always liked Silvie, way before; and he

slept on her couch to stand watch for her. He waz going to take it with her—not Silvie alone, just them both. It really made him wont to wear a turtle neck for her. Silvie she'd been dressing up in a miniskirt for awhile, before all of that/for him.

Zombie and Mark and Mark (Re:Mark is what we call him. Cauze of the two being called Mark) are sittin down wid their chicks. They all don't pay much mind, really, to what's going on about and all. And all I Edison can say is that;

### -I HATE ASIANS-

Zombie laughs. Sparker'z a bit uppset over that,

-Why-

-Because, I waz tryin to make a phone call, before, and dis one just stands there, in my way, and wont move; like he wontz to challenge me or somethin like he'z macc'n fer the evening. I jus plow on by. But the moment waz unnecessary, ya know? He waz just tryin to play up to his nice stad friendz. Fukkin monkey! Thy'r nothing but a group of uppity colonial wanna be'z-

-Cool-

Silvie sayz,

-You're a racist, man.-

I Edison figured—observant, pissed off and a bit drunk. I would apologize for this rant next week, though. But not to that phukwit.

We all decided that since they fired the Finger Mashers, the Grateful Dead cover band wasn't bringing the atmosphere up any. To add to it, the audience waz pretty concerned over our arrival. They were a bunch of fraudulent celtic fukkin preps. A lot of traitorous protestant sellouts who disgrace their fore fathers and moms, and forethat, for a hollywood produced drunken broguish product.

Next week it'd be better—they got these bands playing: The Pricks, the newly reformed, and what we're told, improved, Rubbish Bwoyz, and this Oi band from Edmonchuk called the Cleats. This time the RB'z got this Celtic, Ska, H.C. sound...go figure; Zombie'z playin drums for them too and Gina'z on fiddle. She could play!

We all ended up going to buy some cases and headed back to Sparker'z place. Sparker and me and Zombie and Mark and Re:Mark, we sing, real loud, the Silvertones' "True Confessions," on the way back, and figured the chicks swoon.

I look up and in the corner of the hall, just at the entrance to the living room, is Sparker, in hiz cook outfit, staring at me, smoking a cig. He sayz to me;

-Oi yoi, yush, whatz up? wanna go for a beer? cool-

## Ain't Really Nothin' but a Movie

Never/nvr/nvr/use your own stuff. Bragger fukt up real bad. He started. ...and his body waz gone and so waz his attitude. He could walk round proud and strong no more. He waz like all the bAKRA scagheadz = he dated this trailer park chick. Thats what got it going, I'm pretty sure/that's what got it.

He owed so much to so many bAKRA that he waz nvr going to get out of it. They weren't going to be there when things fell apart, either. Thy're like that = they wonted to see things fall apart. They wonted to see the coon run himself into the ground.

Fukking Steppinfetchit, man//tha's what they wonted. But, Hey! they were his brooooooz. What can you say about that? They got him to get like those guyz on the videoes—geto fab.

They did.

He ditched being a baldhead. Bragger waz a baggy ass. Thy'd all seen *Menace**II**Society*. Bragger waz going to play thy're lead.

Bragger's already walking but he'z already dead.

I waz at this alnight coffee place where all the rapheadz go to pick up at the end of the night. Mostly, glitzy ravy types n dayglo gangsta'z. They got this either bad Mean Streets or Tupac 'body bag' look. He's with the scrubber. She waz all fukt up. I go over.

-Oi, Eddy, you still hear from Prochain? ha...'member dat day-

-Hey, Bragger, looking good-

-*Comme ci comme ça*-

Hiz cow'z almost falling into her coffee.

-Wotz wid her-

-Oh, Eddy, this is my girlfriend Yanncy. You've met her right-

-No, you keep talking about her, but I never met the...her-

Yanncy can speak:

-I was walking into that restaurant on the corner with Bragger, when this native ammmmerican comes over to me and he says...'You Insulted My Girlfriend'...I never met her before and I didn't know what he was talking about. Then He just slams me 6/7 times in the head-

(lIKE a cHELSEA'D tAKE tHAT sHIT)

-I keep telling her we should go to the hospital, But she don't want to go. She might have a concussion-

-Nah, she's got a bump on her head. If you could see the bump, it's not. The lumps got to be on the inside-

I went looking for the fukker cauze I Edison got bad news—my mom died some daze ago, only I found out only taday. You figured she'd been more careful about what she took up in her. You figure she'd know what shit waz too pure. You figure she'd get through it.

I'm pretty sure...it wazn't her first time—I thot it waz her bloodpressure the first few times-when I waz little.

I Edison tossed the dEVILfukker out of my life. It wazn't tuffluv. It waz the smell that waz getting to me.

# RatPatrol

Quex was lying on the sand paper floor. Highball started to tug at his sleeve. Quex was staring at the ceiling. The white room waz smeared with a bunch of shadow from the streetlights—*The Night Porter,* Dirk Bogarde: it's a great film. Vodden had talked about it**called him one night/drunk. He waz with G-d, who brought hiz VCR over. They had been watching it together. He talked about the love and games they had played and the dancer.

Highball was tugging at his shorts. He wonted to show him something. He decided to get up and inspect the negroes in his room. Highball had drawn his attention to something//and in the wink of an eye//he saw each hanged man had something etched on its back//the #'d pages were tattooed to their necks. If he followed each one reading the higher bodies before the lower ones/like a comic book/then he had the story...

✖ ✖ ✖

Prochain walked out of the can after applying vitamin (E) onto his arms.

Elie waz asleep on the couch:

The ratz were all over Elie

The crib waz way small for him. 17 yr old tattooed little fetus, folded up like an accordion inside an old wooden padded rocking baby bed.

They climbed in//btwn his legs/running over his bent arms. A couple of them were biting at this hands.

They were tearing at his hands.

They were tearing at them [bloody lacerating] trying to get inside his veins.

Prochain heard him screaming but did nothing.

He just mumbled//

-Ratz are nice. So I'm told-

...he stroked his head a few times and rolled over on his side and went to sleep.


***Ratz are nice//Ratz are nice***/I said//

pretty rat/pretty/pretty rat/all nice and clean and with little tits//but cutey.

Thy're big and tiny with longy legs

they crawl and rip.


Elie's in the bathroom 1st//cool clear porciline//

Elie walks way out and sees Tim going up to Duppy/stepping over the little chelsearat.

Duppy wonts him to suck on his mouth hole.

# BLaM

Elie sees only 2 parts of a body//just the bottom and there's gooey shit all over his stuff and clothes.

# AAAAAAAAhhhhhhhhh

# hahahahahahahahahahaha-hahahah

and again...

# BLaM

Prochain's stroking his head with a shotgun in his hand—and a baldhead, just behind...

iz humping sacks of wet stuff/out the room/down the hall.

✖ ✖ ✖

Quex ran his hand down the etchings/they were embossed onto the bodies//scars//If he peeled them off/carefully/maybe he'd have them bound into a portfolio.

-Hey Highball, what the fuk, huh, what the fuk-

# Fuk You

There waz a porn on and these monkeyz were watching it in the barracks—once. This bitch waz getting the shit fukt out of her by thiz guy. Quex and Yody and Faggot and some of the other monkeyz/were watching away. Faggot waz Freuding out and cutting pieces off this salami and eating it.

-You know that cunt of an MP that I have to work with-Flücky looked over at Quex and...

-The stoopid bitch-

-The private-

There waz only 1 girl MP on the base but...

-Yeah-

-She'z a cunt-

The guy started jammin the bitch doggy-style and she got louder.

She waz really wet. Thy've got lube too mek it wetter than it really iz.

-Fuk that cuntz stoopid-

Faggot had a wad of salami in hiz cheek:

-She getting to you-

-I don't know how she pasted the fukking crse-

-Thy're letting more femalez in/now-

The bitch waz sucking the fender off the guy/now. She had highheelz and blonde hair.

This guy Jason sayz:

-When doez she do roundz-

-Tomorrow shez by herself-

The guy in the video pullz out and jackz himself off over the bitches face...

-Oh, wow, man, why would a guy humiliate himself like that when he's got a pussy to cum in-

Yody looked disgusted and wonted to turn the video off.

-Next time she doez her roundz we should gang fuk the bitch-

-She doez roundz during the silent hrz-

-You got duty-

-No-

Quex turnz around and starts to take poll as to who's got duty tomorrow night. The tally waz up to 7//it waz a plan.

Tomorrow night/when it came/from a military stand point//
tactically/

       /it waz fukt =

you see

       she waz a military cop
       so the bitch had a gun.

# 4

## My War

## Sometimez I invision bloody legz.

Flücky spent most of a year writing a ltr to hiz mother. It went for pages. He talked about all sortz of shit. Especially why he refuzed to catch a ball. She yelled at him at the gamez/but he just stood there/az the ball went toward him and flopped or hit him in the chest. The other kidz would yell at him/the coach/the scout leader//who he hated. Poor Flücky, he don't do much of nothing. Nobody would talk to him but Yody. They picked him out as the local stay away from. They imaged all sorts of shit about him—nothing true. He walked 'round screwfaced most of the time. Hell, I would too if my momz waz serving time for dealing coke in some backwood trailer park.

…to tell ya the truht—I do.

## I don't know what's, what no more, mom.

It waz a list of shit he waz hoping Yody would read first/before sending it.

It doezn't matter Flücky, zwot Yody said. They were drinking in this field.

We waz on the ground and it got darker. He waz close to me. I like Yody.

He said it didn matter. I think all the time aboutgirlz. I waz thinkn about mods. I read about some stuff. I read in this comic for them. I only picked one up. They spent most of the time talkin about some spy stuff and scooter runs.

Flücky waz thinking he had to contemplate a mod lifestyle cuz,

1. the chicks couldn't stand him,
2. the bootboichail stuff waz getting to be a liability—Quex being so weird lately,
3. he didn't like looking poor—cauze he waz poor and,
4. there waz this guy he played footzy with for awhile. He'd come by and see him at the Armory. He waz just from another company. They shared the same Armory. Flücky favored his vespa. He like the chick that betty'd.

It doesn't matter Flücky.

Yody didn move away when I told

him about contemplating a mod
life style.
   I figured I could change
thingz. I didn't though, I didn
know if Id feel comfortable with-
it. The muzic/etiquette and
money. I don have all that kind of
money. I don like pretendn I do.

Flücky, you don't have to have money to
be...well...ya know. Flücky felt you did. Flücky felt that
you had to act like you did. If not people just won't talk
to you. It doesn't matter Flücky.


That the cutey that I think
about/on the vespa/ We just bat
theze emotional ballz back and
forth//like feet under a table.
Yody sayz/that/G-d doezn have
money/even if he iz wot I think
he iz. He's from a trailer park. As
far as Yody knewit/it waz a family tradition with hiz volk.

   -Oh wow/man/Flücky-
   Yody told Flücky to come here.

*To comeon/to come here.*

Flücky put the pen down/he'd made it to page 48. He pulled hiz legz up onto hiz rack. He remembered/that/az they were on the grass//Yody rested him on hiz chest.

-Just go to sleep-

-Yeah//...//You're not going to snore are you-

-I don't know/Cathy never mentioned anything-

## We've Come To Wreck Everyting:
### *G-tt ist mit uns*

Macho neo-redneck burnout assholez all over. On the stage are big guyz with hoodz. Then no hair. The pit iz full/Vodden stood in the middle of the mess waiting to detonate. Someone/people think/has just sacrificed a baby rat that waz confuzed by the metal and thot that it waz a another construction site going up.

People **Hailed Satan** / People **Sieg Heiled** / some alternated btwn the two. Then there were the guyz like the Dumbdumz that stood against the wall with their armz folded/breathing pissed off heavy and stared. Except for Flücky, he popped and rolled and propelled hiz body into anything that did or didn't move for 1.5 sec. Killer pummeled him//but he still got going//until Sparker dove boot first at hiz head/but that wazn't no matter anyway/so he just kept going. Fightz brokeout—btwn crewz. But the pitt waz so intense/you'd get pulled away and tossed over another part of the bar. If you ended up anywhere near the stage it could mean a human sacrifice. But bouncers and roadies can be like that/especially at a '70s Frampton concert. Actually, thy'd probably, have more girlz there and then that 'groupie' word would pop up. Girliez don't fuk rockstarz anymore/they just start their own bandz.

What took the most gutz waz the baggy ass skater

types that showed//they got surrounded by bruizerz/baldies and long haired alloyed boyz. It waz kind of cute to see. They got slaughtered but it waz still cute to see them trying. They didn't let anymore of thoze kiddlingz in cauze of the bodycount going out//and no more bald people/either.

Vodden stood in the middle.

T'waz the stroboscoptic epileptic nightmare of the led fisted noize and they knowed it.

**✖ ✖ ✖**

Drunk fukz and pissed to hell tired trailz lead out/from there. It's off home tonight—blood and salt— blut and t-shirtz stuffed insided back pocketz = screaming crazy jackassez//too tired/too tired = **fight**:

-Hey, Yody let's go roll those guyz-

-I'm beaming on that Nigger across the street, Flücky -

It waz Sparker.

Would Cathy get wet watching him do it. Prochain crossed the street to go buy a pack of smokes. Flücky waz alwayz acting like a wupper//he waz so fukking jacked. And he and Yody would fall into maniac sink— it waz aggro hooligan Smothers breddas to the fuk.

What they needed was a show that would go on long/hard enough so thy'z could pass out before thy'z could get everyone in trouble. Tonight'z target waz Sparker and Killer.

But would Cathy get wet. You couldn't tell because her and Doris were chatting it up infront of the club/knowing what waz coming up.

-That nigger, there-

It waz Killer.

Flücky and Yody crossed the street and started to tag along behind Sparker and Killer. Sparker and Killer hearz them and what they were saying/real loud/about pulling out an antinigger machine and rommelling them into submission. Sparker and Killer stop walking infront of the junkies begging them for change and a smoke. Killer laughs at the varments—thy're holding a sign that sayz, "Capitalism Work."

Sparker flipped them a coin.

G-d waz watching.

Like a comicbook hero Flücky takes a leap in the air n mashes Sparker dead square in the back. It waz a perfect execution—Flücky landed straight and steady.

Then Yody starts to give Sparker the boot and Killer doez the honourable thing and slamz Yody to the side of the head.

Yody sayz nothing = not a fukking woid. Then/suddenly/Flücky'z body hitz him over and pushes him onto the bum. Sparker waz up and the Dumbdumz weren't no more. Sparker keepz slamming Flücky in the head/badly = badly because//he didn't hit the right way/he waz a scrapper no pug/not him. Hiz knuckle waz out too much and he busted it. Killer n him thot it waz just dislocated. But thy'd find out it waz not/about noon the next day.

-What the fuk Yody/get over here-

Cathy waz or waz not getting wet but she was loud about what she wonted. Doris just walked off with Quex.

-Get the fuk over here-

Yody took a step toward Sparker. Killer booted him in the rib cage [crack]. Cathy ran over.

-You're a phukhead Yody...[Flücky waz getting up]...stay the fuk down-

It waz advice = Killer, he stopt reaching inside his flt for something. Sparker and him, they just booted it out of there.

Yody managed to pull himself up and reach for Cathy but she stepped away.

-Get the fuk away from me-

Yody didn't say nothing.

-You just leave me on the corner like that/I could've have been attacked myself-

✖ ✖ ✖

-I made you this, I wont you to have it-

Elie waz witout Pro, for a while, and goin to meet him, I guess, when he stopt by the stand.

-Geeee, thanks, shugaboo-

He handed me this really gear patch. I mean it was pretty big. What was written, had red and blk outline and was filled in wid screamin blue—was **OXBLOOD.**

-I had time, so I made it-

I'm stoket;

-Thanks-

-I draw and make things, you know-

-Fukkin good...-

-I'm not entirely useless-

He waz a stranger but I'm not a strange land. I Edison wonted to invite him back to the squat.

-Oi yoi, *mais quescön faiz ce soir,* shugaboo? Why don't you come wid-

-I don't know... You really think I sound like HR....-

...just to get him away from sadsack...

-I got to meet...-

-'course, Elie.... Comeon Elie-

-I'm supposed to meet him, anyhow...-

...I rubbed the bristle of hiz head. I wazn't out to skank hiz heart or anything...

**✖ ✖ ✖**

I'm lying on my mat in my tent, I got setup, inside my squat = I hate the wallz of the place. Windowz bug me. It'z got good room in it. Elie could even stand in it and he'z taller than me. Sparker he made me a tape and I got this tape, wid Urban Riot, the Pricks, X, and Impact and it's got Laurel Aitken, Dave Barker, Delroy Wilson, Clancy Eccles, the Specials—all kinds of mixes of shit. Right now, "Pussy Price" is just crankin—I could spare the batteries tonight. I got books all over. I Edison like to keep the one I'm read-ing, the most, by the mat. I got Nikki Giovanni's stuff next to me, tonight and Horatio Alger—Fuk! I luv Paul Hoffmann.

-Ya know Elie, there waz beaucoup de merde in this town, for awhile. Callin up wickedness; tearin shit up. You should have been there. Razzamatazzin heliumheads steppin on toes, not knowing/or caring, who knows/who/what made what. You can't be maccin, or playin like that, Elie. It's gettin better, though. Some started, a few started, hangin' wid street niggaz, putoz and Paki chicks... But it's still here, in a way, alotta fallout, mostly. Thurs, waz da night, and the lads all meet at the pub. It's not organized. It just happens. It's a *bon* crew, not a large one. The most interesting of the lot, I'd say, are Re:Mark, Zombie, and Sparker—and Roadkill, yeah Roadkill...and the chicks—Silvie and Gina. You ever meet them, Elie? nah, huh? There use to be a band, that was cool to watch, that we'd all wait for the next off key note to be hit. It became a tradition to see how far into the set thy'd make it without the singer fukkin it up, and the band drawing out the evening with the 12 min. rendition of the "Guns of Navarone." During one of their sets, Re:Mark got hit in the face by this WP monkey who waz on hiz honeymoon. They were visiting from somewhere. They had some monkey of a backwoods friend wid dem. You know Zombie-

-Yeah, I think-

-He used to ride a board...-

-Yeah, yeah, Prochain, mentions him once in awhile...-

-...yeah, bet he doez.... He ever mention Vodden-

-Yeah-

-Yeah//...//bad juju//...Zombie, he was a skater before he became a Skin, Elie. He became a Skin for all the wrong reasons, Elie.

He played wid the Rubbish Bwoyz. Now, he's wid the Finger Mashers...well, now he'z back wid the RB'z, but it'z a different one now, sorta. The RB'z only new 7 tunes, mostly Oi and a couple of Ska songs and stuff. Ska, being not a music that lasted over 2mins, they had a time coverin a 90min set. We all figured that Thurs. was the time they rehearsed. They got fired, too, just like the Finger Mashers— who were good. I guess it's something about Zombie'z bandz. But he keeps getting chances-

Elie iz fiddling through my tape collection and he'z looking a little thunder struckin—like he'z not that much of a twit.

-You know Elie/it's not that hard to get rid of some-body. People get disappeared all of the time. Someonez walking down the street/drag him in and check him out in an alley. You think every-thing'z like those copshowz = Propaganda, Elie. No body = no one cares//body = no one cares-

Elie, he just keeps starin at the tape in hiz hand. But the way he'z starin, iz like he'z not really lookin at it no more, because it's vanished.

-You're not a celebrity = you heard from Duppy-
I Edison throw him a book by my mat.

-Here/Elie/Blk people only appear on tv when thy're doing foolish thingz-

-Duppy said I'm not geto-

-Who's Duppy, Elie

any one hear from him

anyone/Elie

You still here from Prochain, Elie//

...//It's not bodies, Elie.

It's corpses.

No one important.

You don't exist-

...but unlike me/Elie just runz out of my squat.
I Edison yelled. I really Yelled....

**-DUPPY PLAYED A WICKED GUITAR. HE USED TO SKATE, REAL GOOD, TOO-**

✖ ✖ ✖

When she kissed him she didn't feel it. He wanted to devour her. Yody would slide his tongue down her throat and cram it inside. He'd suck Cathy's tongue back out and she felt like he would bite it off. Like he wanted more/to inhale her insides.

All her life, lately, she didn't feel anything. Cathy figured he was the same because he was so desperate with her in bed. It didn't matter kissing her. It was like being swallowed by a snake with a stolen egg in its belly.

In the movies they saw in school, it always spat out the crushed shell//distort its shape/until the acid dissolved it enough to become the form of the snake or Yody. She pulled out and started laughing.

-What-

-Nothing-

She kept laughing.

He hated when she did that. He pretended to laugh but he hated it. His touch tickled her/and annoyed/but he was a good guy/to hangout with.

Cathy got off him and out of bed and went to the stereo to put on a record.

-Wait what are you putting on-

-Something-

-At this hour-

-At any hour-

-No...-

-It's *Sitting in Limbo*. It's alright-

Yody just lied there looking up at the ceiling like a housewife. The music started and he wanted Cathy back in bed. It waz sure that she didn't want to do anything but she did like getting into bed with him. It was nice lying next to him. He had a nice body. Especially/when he had his clothes on and they were out at the local. She could imagine him better. His every move as he spoke/got excited and lifted himself from the table to get into Flücky's face or something. You'd catch the power of his belt as it poked its way above the table top. She wanted to hold on to it.

It was great imagining him naked after seeing him clothed, knowing it was pretty special that he let her see him that way.

She got excited again and came back to bed desiring something. But then/he touched her and she rolled over and went to sleep.

# The Cement Beach

Elie couldn't believe the grandeur of the architecture. He had his head up looking at the scrapers and noticing that everything, for once, wasn't porcelain. There'z no muzic on the streetz. All you get/iz what comez from peoplez carz az they driveby//life bites of bad top 40 and even worst indie. He kept a good pace with Prochain, who was jacked now that his babe waz back by him. Hiz eyez were crystal and beaming through everyone that looked hiz way. Then that bracket got filled in with a rockstar tough garçoon//skanker...

-Oi, Bragger/Oi yoi...-

Bragger stopped on the corner and was gliding forward//hovering toward Prochain.

-Have you seen Eddy...-

Bragger was slurring//mellow cool.

-No-

He caught a glimpse at Elie.

-Hey, kid-

Elie nodded and kept looking at the sky. Prochain gave Elie a little shove forward and started to cross the street.

-Oi, Prochain, check ça, I've got a present for you-

He takes off to the wall and reaches in his pocket and pullsout a folded paper cone.

-What-

-I only have 3 left. So I can only give you 1-

-What-

-What do you want a white 1 or a blue 1-

-What are they-

-You want a white 1 or a blue 1-

-What are they-

-I don't know-

-Oh, vals-

-I took 1 each [haha...]-

-Iaaaa'llllll taaaaake a blue 1-

-[haha]-

-Thanks-

-T.C.B., man-

Bragger goes hovering off toward the Duggy Tavern, checking out all the show posters pasted against this permaconstruction site—chuckling, lightly.

Prochain is getting off telling Elie how to eat the bacon and cheezeburger, without getting the glop from the filling to fall all over the place, when Elie finally sees that unreal chelsea.

Elie was sitting on the sidewalk munching on his burger and she's sitting on the side walk across the street with a brand new pair of Grinders and T-shirt and flt.

She's still real pretty and has a fat bruised lip. Prochain and her, catch each other's eyez and she starts to get up and walk over to him. But Prochain scurries across the street and they stop dead = on the beach. Prochain's handz start waving and he looks around like a jacked deer. She opens her tiny hand. Then he pullz a 50 out of his pocket and triez to hands it to her. Her hand became a site. I see Kre…'n…and theze guyz—real bruizerz—the new onez—not like the last onez—no coolio—jus dread.

…I Edison tell ya this—they had seen the movie…

# Whoah Yoooooi!

Prochain kissed the polluted beach.

*and I'm down.*

*I feel kickingbootboy* **Que**x**!!!** ?
The bandits were yelling:

# -…Dental plaaaaan-

I'm cold          stop     *my friend*

*you*

The Horde were hooting and wahling
howling and growling//
wolves
yell//laughing = howling = wolves

Zom…**Oph!**
were….I liked you *Quex*

# ratchet
### and...

boots.

Elie seez
Prochain's face
suddenly become
a big
clear
blud clat.
I think they stopped
I can't remember after that
wazn't important anyhow.
I do know, all I knowz that Quex, tells me that my jacket looks a lot better, now, wid this patch. Said I Edison
had good taste. Said that the Templars would be even
better. ...said he knowz that, that this one patch and the
jacket mean more to me—gave me beaucoup de dunza
for shining hiz boots.

Nikki could have told Faggot that.
'In the beginning waz the woid and the woid waz...nig-
ger', ya dope.

### *Taken care of business, baby!*

## bLAM bLAM.

-Kiss me neck...-

5

**Aim !**

You envisioned reality and realized you can't deal
With it.
Bring out the thompson gunners!
Here they come
The bloodz—nah/no
Gudolebwoyz//ratpatrolz
Coming seconds after they cleaned up.
The other onez
The new onez
Like the olbwoyz

                Figure

Alwayz

                Right after

That maybe
They should use a jimmybag for this mess = so they
could
Forget sooner
But the effort of reaching over and getting 1 runz too
Much of an effort.
    From coolz to gang to thug = uncool death.
    They tried to keep it together
But too much agressivity iz wearing
When you got to look down at…allathe time.
    All the time
A life
It'z to only ever pay or get paid for it.

# Homocide

Vodden waz bucked and over wet. The extra army parka sweated him up. He hadn't changed in a week since the show...finding out Quex waz gone, didn't help matters much.

I got a Rutger standard automatic

I got a North & Cheney Flintlock

I got a Winchester/70/westerner

     Do you want to see it//

Vodden took hiz parka off and stretched/carefully/he didn't want to break the seal.

The stoopid cow waz asleep and so waz it.

I got a Mac 10

I got a Glock 17

I got a Hi Power = 13 shot-9mm

     You want to see them

He sat himself down in the beanbag chair and felt the adhesive girdle constrict hiz breathing.

I got a Savage 110-MC

I got a Winchester Model 12//field...

I got a Winchester 42

     Do you want to see 'em

He felt the sticky cloth and pressed the tape around hiz stomach and chest. He had the 8 sec. delay detonator = blasting cap and transit cap...

I got a Cobray M-11

I got a Frontier Colt

...a Dragon Colt

...a Hall Breechloader

You want to see it

The nailz wobbled along hiz body like ripped abs.

He could image the smell of the M5's = 8 = 8 = 88

I got a Tec-9

I got a Browning .380

S&W .38//40 model

...a Colt Govt. automatic//45 model

It waz a good show no one's going to ban me.

I'm fukking here

I'm fukking here

...no one fukking banz me

-**NALENE**...-

Dumby criez//she don't wake.

...what do you want to do Nalene/fuk or something? G-d'z alone.

I'm here/knowitwazagood/show.

...should've been there...

✖ ✖ ✖

Elie took hiz eyez off of him. He left Bragger bab-bling and happy. He'd just about cleaned him out.

He walked faster and faster.

*I don't unnerstand this world/*

the razor cut into hiz fore arm.

it waz really cold out so it numbed the pain...

*I don't understand this world/*

at all...

Quex is Quex.

*Eddy IS.*

He started cutting deeper and running.

He found a wall by a closed cig store and sat there/on the beach/ cutting away.

The blood cameout more and more all along hiz body.

He opened hiz shirt and started to cut there//too.

Bragger'z stuff waz the good stuff. He took it and dumped 2 match headz on hiz tongue and started to rub the rest into the cutz.

Who the fuk am I

✖ ✖ ✖

They finally let me see him. He had a room with otherz. One guy waz this guy who had been caught running down the street naked with a pentagram carved on hiz chest. He waz waiting for hiz boyfriend to pick him up and bring him back to the country. Hiz boyfriend waz a radical fairy. He just didn't own him and when he had decided to take off to the city/what could the fairy do. But he waz still coming for him.

He waz telling me and Elie how the medz were fukking up hiz head. So he went to take a bath to calm down. It waz then when we were alone. The best peo-ple were in that ward. They just couldn't reconfigure the woild to mek all the bad thingz not exist. It didn't matter what they were…you didn't have to be Blk to be a Nigger no more.

He waz all bandaged up and dopey. He could only move hiz head around and smile to see me.

-Eddy-

-Hi, shugaboo-

He tried to raise hiz hand up to me. So I took it.

-Ain't they got no shame, Eddy-

-Now-

-Ain't they got no shame-

He had charcoal all over hiz mouth. They dumped it in him to separate the shit in him from being abzorbed.

-Come live with me-

-ain't they got no shame-

-What you wont-

-…no shame-

-…be still-

-…ain't they got no…-

-So mek to fight. Fight the friggin monkeyz, man. You saw—We fight-

-…they don't have any…-

-No-

The guy came out of the tub with a towel round hiz waist. He looked good = even with the pentagram. He said:

-Here…-

…and he walked quickley to hiz bed table. He came

back with a match book. On it were theze markingz = circlez and squiggley stuff.

He gave it to Elie and told him too hold on to it.

-It'll keep you safe-

He touched my shoulder and went to get dressed. Nudity wazn't a problem with him.

Elie had the hyrogliphics in his hand and even managed to take it up to his face to look better.

-If I were you//I'd take him out of here-

He walkz back up to me with a guitar in hiz hand.

-Thy're fukt/I'm schizo but thy're fukt-

He waz walking out the room =

-That stuffs gonna keep you safe it's Irish-

-Well, hold onto it/El-

I Edison move close to hiz ear and whisper/while touching the stubbly sidez of hiz head:

-Duppy waz never no gud anyhow—but family'z....Can I hold you/Elie...I swear/I wan't hurt yer armz-

6

Perhaps…

I Edison think.

They say Blk absorbz all light. Sparker sayz, he drawz him and Killer in hiz mind. So it'z filled wid them all. It's better than television or moviez. Wot'z Sparker'z subject: Killer//ras enuff to be on that tree of life of hiz n hiz familiez', buddiez absorb'n light.

*No internal damagez, much. He clawed, for awhile...no pain, no trouble—not much Killer and the crew would'n be able to handle... he's all apart, part nothin and pulped on concrete now—jus blud clat, I guess.*

...never tell

Sparker counts down the cash from the parlourz take that day.
He seez Killer and that one good eye.
Killer, he got a patch now//makes him look dread—dread luey.

Killer waz slumpin on the couch watching the speakerz move to the whacky keyboardz of *Eastwood Rides Again*. Hiz neck pushin hiz head forward and back in total perpetuation. Sparker wonted/Sparker did wont/to go on over to him/to get closer.

Killer sayz he keeps Sparker on the top of hiz head and he starts to dream. Hiz head gets filled with a slow shuffle//a skank and hop. True rebels now, united, moon hopping yush…come forth!

Done ciphering/
in an act of imagination/
   …you thank your new venture for all the laughs n pain/
   hurt n fun it would bring forth
         and summon up a holocaust/
   and thoughts of:
Nikki,
The Wild Bunch,
Upsetters,
Rhygin, Oxblood, 'n' Alger—in total praise-
and Killer'z
and Sparker'z
and their
crepuscular heart(s) exploded
infinitesimally
explode in honour.

He'z [M] fren like the sparks in my hed.
I Edison try to get back to Sparker.
To grab hem close…
Killer beats me to the punch;
   -Yush, Com'ere, letz get some sleep. I'm fukkin bagged-

**✖ ✖ ✖**

Elie decided to let hiz hair growout into baby dreads. No big deal—hiz trip—he always liked HR, anyway. He don't hang, too much, wid me n the Ruffy breddaz. He still gets into the music—same buddy. He layed off doing anything for over a year.

In bed, I Edison get scared people are going to hurt me. Elie got taught by bAKRAZ to numb all that out with phukhead stuff. I Edison sleep better. We sleep well. We're like carnals/bluds. We're breddaz. We walk like loverz. Stay away from poofstaz and tweakerz.

With Elie in my life, now, it's all so warm. Hiz skin iz still smooth. He patz and strokes me on hiz canvas. We got a candle going. It's not non too safe to do that— but we favor it better than electric. Mr. Edison's too expensive anyhow. Elie's got the patent on this one. I Edison hear him breathe and it's copacetic—slow and peace like.

My head bobbs from the vibrations of his chest against the floor.
He smiles inside.
I Edison
Myself
Laugh to sleep and wakeup the same.

Elie doez nice pictures. You should see them, daddy. He waz in art class, before he became a milk carten kid and they said he wazn't going to go anywhere. He's doin me another tat, special, tomorraw. He made me a pretty good one a couple of weeks ago. He used spray paint and crayon and gouche to get a bigger version on the window of the shop. A part of me iz up in all glory, now.

There'z a club we go to and thy've got speed painting contests. Elie can paint sooper aggro thrash. When, we're in need of throw away dunza, he goez and winz— t.c.b., yush. People come up to him to mek him some offers—alwayz more, now. Elie doesn't want to get used up like Basquiat waz done to. Like he waz, before, over there, with the bAKRAZ...

I like Elie's drawingz. He drawz the Rudies n Moonstomperz we meet at places = clubz n pubz, on the streets, all the crew—toojoo tuff. He could do a sooper book that's trey bon, that's trey ruff, that's trey tuff, like our heartz and pride. It'd be better than television or movies. I Edison remember all this stuff. He's got stuff, of me n the crew up in the parlour. I Edison see a painting of Quex. I Edison wonder if he's still grumpy—where the fuk he iz—never tell. A promise iz a promise. ...sorta hope he's happy, wid no fear—chasing the daemonz I Edison conquered.

-'Rite Highball-

...I swear...

**✖ ✖ ✖**

Some of the Horde were playing pool and waiting for Cyco's turn up in Elie's chair. They were missing Quex a bit.

But such iz the life of a hooligan—what goes around comes around—ya know. Elie's az good, if not better. They still had Quex's tapes//audio art//screaming speeches of him and Highball, all intoned like the **Psychopathic G-d**—hiz favorite book. They were throwing back 40 ouncers, like the way he would have wonted it. Zombie wonted hiz tat mag back and the brand he had lent him. He wazn't prepared to ask the copperz.

Cyco, Zombie, Mark, and Re:Mark were listening to this tape they had found in Quex's office. It waz a of a chugger or someone imitating one—sounded like he waz the guest at a boot party. Must have been Yody who dubbed in the music and noize. Those guyz had the accents down pretty good. Real Amos and Andy classic stuff. It drowned out the buzzing from Elie's gun running in the next room.

S o o p i r coule**the joint waz, now. Muggz like us = Sparker and Killer and me/I Edison, we could trust Elie much better with the designs. Bronze/brass n copper takes ink different—Quex had an idea but El knowz.

Cyco, Zombie, Mark, and Re:Mark were playing a wicked game of pool since their babes had left. Crystal meth and speed balls//wicked, wicked, wicked//slam/claque/thunk//

-Yeah, yeah, he does it and sinks-

-Scratched-

-Blk's right there-

Discussion started**Cyco and Re:Mark//borders and games//

    -White remains Re:Mark-
    -I like to keep the eightball-
    -White remains to the end-          **scratched**
    -I keep the blk-                    **phonograph//**
    -White-                             **crackle//pop**
    -I'll play it this way-             **//snap**
    -We have to be the same-
Mark stepped in;
    -Teamwork my breddas, it doesn't work otherwise-
    -I hate sports, Re:Mark-
    -...stop watching Chomsky-
    -...stop reading books-
    -I like books. I like watching Chomsky-
    -He hates sports-
    -He's a jew = Jews hate sports because they can't play sports-
    -Because they read books-
    -Black balls//jews and books = you're a Dumbdum aren't you Re:Mark-
    -No more than you're a buller, Cyco-
    -Can we take this shit off. It sucks-
Re:Mark stood there with his Q tor'd up and,
    -Put Oxblood on. I like Oxblood-
    -Why don't you put on the Subway Thugs and maybe we could get a repeat performance from Roadkill-
Re:Mark sunk a ball so hard the white went across the

room and nuked a rat. Elie came out into the hall with Kreege. Roadkill waz following, just behind. The adrenaline waz rushing him. He waz pulling on hiz freddy, ever so slowly, and Roadkill, he hollers:

### -"Let's show a little reverence you bastards"-

Elie thot it waz funny;

-If you bandits would stick a crowbar in your wallets and spare some change, maybe you could get the rest of the ballz n play a real game one day. Cyco, get in here. I got Edison coming in in an hr-

-Wot the hell can you do in an hr? Eddy can cue up—hang for awhile. Wat?! he some V.I.P., now-

-Kiss me neck, Cyc. I don't think that's goin to happen, yush. I could bump you, you know-

-Nah, nah, it's OK MON. We go fe mek de tattoo-

-Fuk you! Cyco. Sparker can afford the lawsuit if I fuk up. ...Oi! bredda, Zombie! ...could you tek that shit off. It's fukkin disturbing-

**Author Notes:**

**Over 5 mins. of noize, loneliness, comic books,
television, talkshow politics, and murder:**

**1.** *…it's like a fresh tattoo, if you print a page. It captures a moment/place, sentiment, and period. It orchestrates the body in motion as it flexes to move a pen/strike at a key/form a fist/lift a drink or move to a rhythm. The words become the unspoken intertextuality of ethnic, racial, and cultural metaphoric speech. The metre of casual dialogue = a rhythm/noise/visual/bass, a soundtrack to a postliterate train of thought.

…a printer ejects swatches of stolen tissue that collects the sound and images of what is considered low brow art and skill//

Hardcore (H.C.)/Country/Rockabilly/Oi
Thrash and Speedmetal/Rap/Deathmetal/Blackmetal
Cinema/Television and;
Comic Books

**88 (or 1488):** "H" being the eighth letter of the alphabet, 88 has come to symbolize the phrase "Heil Hitler." A paranoid, WP, late 80s early 90s catchphrase used by monkeys and boneheads (esp. militia types). Similarly, the number 18, where 1 = A and 8 = H (as in Combat 18) stands for Adolf Hitler. 88 and 1488 are used as a signature or salutation, mostly by Cyber Skins. The "14" in 1488 comes from the "14 Words" (We must secure the existence of our people and a future for White Children), a slogan attributed to David Lane (Wothenson) of the Order (die Bruder Scweigen), an offshoot of the W.C.O.T.C. and Aryan Nations. These individuals were a small group headed by Bob Matthews (now deceased) who used racist theory as a justification for murder and theft. The Order's activities, especially after Matthews's death, influenced the Pacific Northwest's WP movement, especially through recruitment of teenage boys in small towns (such as Zombie and Vodden in the text of the book) during the late '80s and early '90s.

**Aitken, Laurel:** His career has spanned from the original Ska, Rock steady, Two Tone scenes through the '90s. His most notable hits—"Everybody Suffering," "Scandal in Brixton," "Jesse James," "Woppi King," "Landlords & Tenants," and "Pussy Price"—were during the Rock Steady and Reggae years. He's always F.A.B.! Simply put: The Boss Skinhead.

**Alloyedboy:** A banger, head banger, a metalhead. Also, a neoredneck burnout; a contemporary North American term for a cooler redneck, with style, who is young, male, and favors heavy metal/deathmetal.

**Anti-Heroes:** From Atlanta, Georgia. Along with The Templars and Oxblood, one of the top American Oi bands. They are noted for their shock value, post-'80s, tabloid, redneck lyrics, and catchy punk sound.

**Antinigger machine:** A baseball bat, blackjack, or oppressive mechanism or force. Also, radical forces merging in order to combat any oppressive mechanism that would attempt to reduce a Black man to the status of a nigger; the physical and mental fight for freedom (and example of which would be Public Enemy's "Black Steel in the Hour of Chaos.")

**Arty:** A military abbreviation for artilleryman.

**Babylon:** The oppressive world of slavery, slave labour, the system. Also, whatever gets you down and tries to steal your pride.

**Bakra:** A West Indian term for a white person. Also, devil, blue-eyed devil; Afro-American/Nation of Islam for a white person or oppressive figure.

**Bard Faust (aka Bard Eithun):** Drummer for the true Norwegian Blackmetal band Emperor. He was sentenced to 14 years for vandalism, church burning (once a popular pastime for the inner circle of blackmetalists—not to be confused with the burning of Southern Black churches in the United States), and the stabbing death of a homosexual acquaintance outside the Olympic Park in Lillehammer, Norway.

**Basquiat, Jean-Michel:** Graffiti and abstract expressionist artist and creator of a character called SAMO (Same Old Shit). Born in Brooklyn December 22, 1960, died August 12, 1988. His work combined the D.I.Y. sensibility of hip-hop and the madness/sarcasm of the post-Dr. King generation of young Blacks in America.

**Battybwoy:** West Indian term for a homosexual. Also, bullerz, manicou—used in the contemporary meaning of "gay," meaning useless, pointless, stupid. "Ofay" is the equivalent Afro-American term, and "puto" (pussy) is the equivalent Spanish term.

**Beerslut:** A person with no pride who will sit, share (most likely mooch) a beer with anyone; has no loyalty or self-respect.

**Bennett, Ronnie (a.k.a. Ronnie Spector):** From the early '60s girl group the Ronettes. She was the ultimate sex kitten from the New York school of street dance (a go go), which came from the Phil Spector and Ellie Greenwich hit factory of teen, Tin Pan Alley, and urban pop. The Wall of Sound's main vocalist, right next to the great Darlene Love.

**Berry Gordyism:** Berry Gordy was founding father and patriarch of Motown (Hitsville, USA), a hit factory that produced the sound of the streets. A term used to describe taking something of your own, developed out of oppression, packaging it, and selling it to the oppressor as the real thing. A way of turning the tables and working your way out of a fix using what you've got—your *kopf* (head).

**Blasphemy:** Blackmetal band from Vancouver, B.C., Canada with a Skinhead and Satanic Skinhead following. Noted for their photo shoot in Ross Bay Cemetery featuring the flaming gravestones of Victoria, BC, pioneers.

**Boichails:** Irish Gaelic for boy (for uses here, see bwoy).

**Bonehead:** At one time this was the name given to a rowdy skinhead, someone who liked to drink and/or fight. The current meaning is a nonthinking person; a WP/Nazi/fascist posing as a Skinhead.

**Bredda:** Originally, a Rude Boy term for a fellow Rude Boy, now used by Skinheads as well. A close *confrère*. Not used casually.

**Bring come (carry go bring come):** To gossip. A term made popular in the Justin Hinds song of the same name and by the U.K. Two Tone band the Selecters, with singer Pauline Black.

**Buffalo soljahz:** U.S. American Indian term for a Black soldier. Brave, stout of heart.

**Butler, Rev.:** Reverend Richard Butler from Hayden Lake, Ida., head of the Christian Identity Movement (Boneheads, WP, Militia).

**Butthole Charlie:** Military term for a homosexual.

**Camms:** Camouflage combat pants (full length or cut at the knee) for the "Bushwhackers" WWF look. They became popular during the militia and HC rap period in North America. Now it's just typical gear for North American Skins, Skaters, and Gangstas, along with the Travis Bickle (*Taxi Driver*) combat jacket psycho look— radical chic. Rapheads (Gangsta) and Wiggers tend to favor flight, FBI, and SWAT flack jackets, and other forms of puff jackets.

**Cappo:** U.S. gangster term for lead gang member—da big guy!

**2.** *McLuhan would argue the global village: Technology is good—the book people are lacking in the rich grammar of the TV = This is referred to today as the postliterate generation— John Gage's bastard children turn to violence and the acoustic space of video and computer games and the delicacy of words typed over television screens.

    ...Wordcore, Jamaican dub poetry, Rap and Rock Steady

are disposed to the Homeric boasts and catalogues of post-modern thugs/hoodlums and desperadoes w/ the hope of kindness and compassion. If you hear the structure of Michael Pendars's poetry or Wanda Coleman's or Chuck D's or Patti Smith's or Michael Turner's or Jim Carroll's or Exene Cervenka's, you'll see a tattoo and note well, that some words are//

-Rhythm
-Lead and
-Bass

**C'est too bon [say too bow]:** it's all good (copacetic) Quebecois/Joile/Creole/Cajun/patwa/patois, jesting street French, spoken with a mixture of English and French words. A corruption of various Euro languages in order to confound. Other examples are: "Check ça" [chek sa] meaning "look at that" or "check it out"; "Comme ci comme ça" [come see come sa] meaning "not too bad"; "Conard" [coo'nard] meaning "bastard"; "Parléd a woid of anglaiz" meaning "spoke a word of English"; "Too joo" [toujours] meaning "always"; "Très bon" [trey bow] meaning "very good"; "Trey" [très] meaning "very"; and "Mais quescön faiz ce soir" [May kes cau faiz sir swa] meaning "So what are we up to tonight?"

**Chelsea:** A Skinhead girl; a super boss chick.

**Christie, Douglas:** From Victoria, BC, Canada, a lawyer,

leader, and lecturer with a large following in the Pacific Northwest. His followers favor extreme right-wing and/or fascist politics and campaigns, organized under the banner of freedom of speech. His most famous clients are Eckville, Alberta secondary school teacher James Keegstra, who was charged with promoting hatred, and Ernst Zundel (see "Zundel, Ernst") who promoted the notion that the Holocaust was a hoax (see "Holohoaxer").

**Chugger/Chug:** Pacific Northwest impolite term for a Native American. Based the stereotype of excessive alcohol consumption.

**Cleats, the:** Edmonton, Alberta, Canada, rhythm and boots music (a.k.a. Canadian Oi) band, also noted for being football/soccer enthusiasts.

**C.O.:** A corrections officer; a prison guard.

**Copacetic:** U.S. '20s and '30s gangster term for "things are real cool." The Rulers recorded a Rock Steady song of the same name.

**Crew:** Similar to "posse" and "wolfpack." An '80s hip-hop term for your gang, your friends. Also, now commonly used by Skinheads to refer to a district or close members of their circle or brotherhood. "Wolfpack" is the more thuggish version, and is commonly used by both the HC/Gangsta crowd (rapheads) and Skinheads.

**Crombie:** A velvet-collared, single-breasted, fly-front, Edwardian or Mississippi riverboat gambler's or gentleman gunslinger's suit jacket or the sports jacket worn to complete the zoot suit. It is commonly called a frock coat or chesterfield. Donning it has the same importance as the sharkskin and is just as taxing on the dunza (money). It can be made of any cloth. It's got an appearance that can look like one of a few things—The Duke in *The Alamo* or *The Shootist,* Doc Holiday and the Earp brothers, or a wicked Edward James Olmos in *Zoot Suit.* So the jacket's got some pretty snorky effects and sure don't make a fella look like no huckleberry—Justice is coming! (For a good idea of the appearance and transformative qualities of the jacket, the 1981 film *Zoot Suit,* written and directed by Luis Valdez and starring Edward James Olmos, about the persecution of a Chicano gang during the 1940s, is a good start. It shows the jacket and the wearers in all their power, pride, and glory.)

**Cullen, Countee:** Groundbreaking Harlem Renaissance Black poet, born in New York City, May 30, 1903, died January 9, 1946.

**Dammack/Macc'n/Mack:** The best, kingpin, a pimp. The most notable use of the term occurs in the Blaxploitation film *The Mack,* starring Max Julien and Richard Pryor. Used here in jest for someone who thinks material things are a sign of success. A consumer, Gangsta rap/general music video byproduct.

**Don:** Top mobster, patriarch of the of the crew (see **Gorgon**).

**Dread:** Dangerous (as in the Ducky Boys, a New York Irish street gang in Richard Price's novel *The Wanderers,* published in 1974); a frightening cool (see **Don, Gorgon, Rude Bwoy**); a fear or bad feeling.

**Dunza:** Cash.

**Edmonchuk:** Canadian term for Edmonton, Alberta, Canada because of its large Ukrainian population and pride in its excessively large Easter egg. Also the home of the Cleats.

**Everett, Betty:** Late '50s–early '60s R&B singer/song-writer with a howling voice.

**Fishbone:** Ska/funk band from Los Angeles/Hollywood around the Two Tone era. Still fronted by saxman, singer, and poet Angelo Moore (a.k.a. Dr. Madd Vibe).

**Garçoon:** Irish Gaelic for a lad, used here in a pejorative sense.

**Geto/Geto Fab:** U.S., South Central Los Angeles, Afro-American term for ghetto—an area in which people are restricted and separated due to class and/or cultural differences from the powers in charge—inner-city concentration camps. Also, depending on the context and intonation, someone who is not a poseur, or someone who has given up and blindly follows the prescribed rules of order, conduct, socializing, and dress of a community—either way, geto is a state of mind.

**Giovanni, Nikki:** A supercool '70s Black poetess; the matriarch of Slam Poetry.

**Gorgon:** Same as "Don," but inspires dread (see dread) and has more street credibility.

**Got/Get Disappeared:** To vanish by means other than your own free will; an unplanned permanent, no frills or thrills, big vacation—as in Jimmy Hoffa.

**Gutterskin (punk):** A scruffy street-level Skin or punk (definitely not from the suburbs and never a middle-class mind-set); a "Raggaslacker" is the Rudie version. Can be a term of derision or endearment—the have nots. Similar terms are *Crusty* and *Crustypunk*.

**Harrington/Harry:** A light jacket with a Stuart tartan lining. Something like what James Dean wore in *Rebel Without a Cause*.

**3.** *A word can be the hums or bops in the background as when a funk musician beats the strings w/ his thumb. It gets tied into the paragraph. Some words take on the repetitive ecstatic riff of ska or reggae or the decay of the crash/noise of H.C. or metal, even Oi. They recline on the page or in the air as if they were all going to amount to a junkie's last sigh. Instead, they collapse into the lost, disorientated, and somewhat satisfied image of Orson Welles after thrashing a room at Xanadu.

**H.C. (HC, Hardcore):** The name of a louder, faster, and street level form of punk rock, often having an accelerated rockabilly beat. The sound originated in Los Angeles, California. It began at the end of the 1970s and carried through to the early '80s. H.C. offset the U.K. and corporate invasion of the music scene and the onslaught of Reaganomics—both politics and mindset. It was created by West Coast musicians like X, Circle Jerks, the Germs, Chris D, the Blasters, and Black Flag. H.C. hustled across North America to influence the underground music scene, even in places like Texas (with the Big Boys), Atlanta (with Georgia's Angry Samoans), Washington, D.C. (with Bad Brains and S.O.A.), and Montreal (with S.C.U.M., Genetic Control, and Fair Warning). As England pogo'd, North America slam-danced.

In the United Kingdom, the Oi compilation *Strength Thru Oi* had been released. With its all-White, all-male following and toying with fascism, it opened a gateway of murky and threatening possibilities. But in the United States *Let Them Eat Jelly Beans* came out and in its own way served as a counterpoint to *Strength. Let Them Eat Jelly Beans* followed in the footsteps of the *Decline of Western Civilization* film and sound track, which had introduced the wit and sound of the Los Angeles H.C. scene to the rest of the U.S. underground. H.C. criticized the "conspicuous consumption" of the time and introduced a back-to-basics style of cropped hair, T-shirts, and Levi's—a prototype North American Skinhead antistyle reminiscent of James Dean or Brando without the ducktail but with all the rebellion. Because the wider exposure of Reggae in North America was through the Rastafarian Roots Reggae explosion, the Skinhead movement had its beginnings in both the Two Tone and H.C. scenes, with H.C. opening the door for the distinct North American Skinhead movement (see **Ving, Lee**).

The battle began between the U.S. and U.K. scenes. The United Kingdom had gone NF (fists and fascism) and New Wave/New Romantic/Techno pop (eyeliner and rock star posturing). The U.S. punk and H.C. bands found the U.K. groups inaccessible. Also, H.C. had less to do with violence and the glorification thereof than it had to do with social realism. Neo-Nazism was not even on the table. H.C. brought Blacks and Latinos back into the underground rock scene (with Bad Brains, the ska-ish Bus Boys, Suicidal Tendencies, members of the Dead Kennedys (DKs), and Black Flag, to name a few). Earlier, the New York funk and rap scene had begun opening the doors with Sugar Hill, Tommy Boy, and, later, with Def Jam. But in this case Blacks, Whites, and Latinos started to play in H.C. bands, reintroducing Reggae and various other influences to the movement.

The scene was trying to escape from the suburban trappings of Reaganomics, but as happened in the United Kingdom to the Oi scene, jocks (yobs, monkeys, boneheads) got the wrong idea and began getting off on the violence. Rather than encourage this behavior, the bands broke up or changed musical direction. X stopped performing the song "Johnny Hit and Run Pauline," which was actually condemning a serial rapist but was sadly mistaken by jocks to be a date rape anthem. Thrash/H.C. band the Dead Kennedys broke up because of government objections to the band's name and freethinking message. The DK's did manage to push the musical assertion "Nazi Punks Fuck Off" before calling it a day.

Enter the Aryan Nations, W.A.R., Resistance, and still more, to spread their trash message of blind nationalism, false pride, violence, and bigotry. The Skinhead history was revised. It was made to appear to be hate-mongering, right-wing, for White males only, middle-class, and paramilitary. And with such standards, the ranks increased to welcome a very sorry lot. The Skins are no longer bonded by brotherhood but by hate. 'Zines such as *Maximum Rock 'n' Roll* and *Flip Side* in the United States and *Hard as Nails* in the United Kingdom held fast and took up the fight. The 'zines still support the H.C., punk, and Skinhead culture (respectively). They continued to assert the fact that the scenes were not part of mainstream or fascist politics, but were and continue to be antiestablishment youth movements fueled by music, style, and rebellion.

Speedmetal and Thrashmetal emerged and ripped the H.C. scene to shreds—faster, louder, harder, and scarier lyrics. (Slayer led the way). Later, a lot of the true believers found themselves involved in not only metal but spoken word, publishing, country music (via Cowpunk and Rockabilly—as in Rank and File and The Blasters), roots rock and roll, Emocore, East Coast hip-hop culture, and even the Los Angeles H.C./Gangsta Rap scene.

At a time in which the music scene and the Skinhead movement were being divided by the likes of Ian Stuart and the NF (in the United Kingdom), Los Angeles Hardcore (in the United States) offset the jock/monkey behavior. H.C. reclaimed punk as an American invention and was an influence for the pre-bonehead period of the North American Skinhead. It developed the concept of multiracial bands (as Two Tone did in the United Kingdom). New York City, for the first time in a long while, was not leading the way (as in Patti Smith, James Chances, Richard Hell, The Ramones, Blondie...). However, the city's scene would return, much later, with Agnostic Front, the Cro Mags, Murphy's Law, and Warzone; and again, with the rise of American Oi, with bands such as the Templars, Bottom of the Barrel, Urban Riot, and Oxblood.

Canada, unfortunately, allowed itself to surrender to the fascist beerhall nationalist mentality by overidentifying itself with and becoming the main supplier in North America of WP music and propaganda. (See **Christie, Douglas, Odin's Law, Rahowa,** and **Zundel, Ernst.**) Dissidents in cities such as Montreal, Toronto, Manitoba, and Vancouver tried to fight the good fight by attempting to hold to the true spirit of the Skinhead movement through punk, Ska, Reggae, H.C., and Oi. But for the time being, the West Coast's new music breathed life into the underground with its return to the rock and roll sensibility.

The early period is, somewhat, chronicled in the Penelope Spheeris films *Decline of Western Civilization* (part one) and *Suburbia*.

The term also means really serious, no fooling around, intense.

**4**. *The Comic Book uses frames and juxtaposition to connect the disconnectedness of thought and words, be it through the gruff noireness of Frank Miller, Dave Sim, or Martin Wales' *Kinder Nacht* or the smooth lines, colours, and ruff justice of Todd McFarlane. They collect the street sounds and activities the way Rap culture manipulates and emulates, via spin art and samples, the ready made terror of interurban life. To frame is to make perfect the moment of the fingers striking the keys which can be the repetition of words and phrases = outlets ripping and shredding, w/ the Knowledge that framing is certainly an attempt to make perfect, to make the words as enticing and elegant as the bovine euphony of a fascist's goose step.

**Holohoaxer:** Anyone who professes that the Nazi Holocaust never occurred. (See **Zundel, Ernst.**)

**Hoochy girls:** A boss, old school, super stripper—someone Charles Bukowski would dream about—sometimes used as a term of derision meaning a tramp.

**Homocide/Homicide:** A nasty crime. Also a lethal form of heroin—twisted.

**Horatio Alger:** Born January 13, 1834, died July 19, 1899. He wrote many a rags-to-riches, hard-working-young-man-makes-good story.

**HR:** Lead singer of the Washington, D.C.–based super-fast, Hardcore punk/reggae band Bad Brains ("Pay to Cum"). The founding father of the D.C. H.C. scene. Not until the Bad Brains was there a H.C. scene outside of the West Coast. If it weren't for the Bad Brains, SOA (Henry Rollins's first band, before joining Black Flag), and/or Ian Mackay (Minor Threat) would not have existed. Rollins would still be working in a pet store. In a way, HR is responsible for Henry Rollins. HR is noted for his razor-sharp, nasal, ear-piercing voice.

**Impact:** French-speaking Oi/H.C. band from Boucherville, Quebec, whose music is often fast and very much in the style of H.C. The torpedoes for DSS Records. They are also noted for doing the occasional Ska tune. More rhythm and boots music and Sooper Cool!

**Indio:** Psychotic antagonist in the Sergio Leone film *For a Few Dollars More* (similar to Prochain in this book). The movie title was reused for a Reggae classic release by Lee "Scratch" Perry and the Upsetters.

**Jojo [yoyo, yai yo]:** Blow, uptown, cocaine.

**Jonesing:** To beg, to be desperate.

**Kind/er:** From the Old English meaning nature. Also, from the German meaning child. Used here to denote and adoptive or natural family, close relations, or race/culture.

**Kinderwhore:** A twinky or teen girl with a Lolita complex. Most likely a skanky chick.

**Labba labba:** To talk excessively.

**Lil'bitch:** An especially nasty male who's petty and disrespectful. Someone who will go out of his way to spiritually, emotionally, and psychologically hurt someone for the attention and the thrill of it; mean-spirited, bad-minded, into the sport of hurting somebody.

**Luey:** U.S. gangster term for second in command.

**MacNeil, Rita:** A folkish middle-of-the-road singer from the east coast of Canada held in high regard by

Ultra-Canadians. Also a CBC Radio and TV personality.

**Madcrazy:** A punk, cool, uncontrollable, H.C.

**Mallrat:** A middle- to upper-class teenager or twinky who favors hanging out in shopping malls.

**Mills Brothas:** The Mills Brothers are a trio of snorky crooners from the 1940s.

**Mod(s):** Abbreviation for modern(s). An early-'60s youth movement (closer to the Rude Bwoy period) coming mostly from the middle classes. The movement prides itself on perfect dress, scooters, and attaining the consumer dream of style and status—basically, 20th century dandies.

Mods have a habit of "slumming" to get to where the fun is. Lower classes have the advantage of being hep to the latest street-level music trends and fashion. Mods tend to take from the latest geto chic, adapt it to fit their class structure, and put it in shop windows in the desire to bring it upmarket. The Rude Boys brought to the United Kingdom their Ska and Rock Steady, and Afro-Americans exported their Motown sound and style. All were quickly picked up by the Mods. This was and is a problem; their parents and "square" members of their class didn't and still don't understand or approve of this geto chic.

Mods have always been elite. They look for style,

are very much into fashion, and change completely with the times—even going back to the early 1900s where these gilded youths were referred to as "bright young things."

It's a young consumer culture (20th century post-war teen rebellion). As the '60s progressed, the three-button-suit–wearing, scooter-riding Mods went upmarket again, adopting flashy psychedelic wear (as in The Who) as their own. The Monkey suit disappeared—ruffles and Beau Brummels arrived. The early to mid '60s period is the best known Mod era because of its combination of White and Black working-class style and the media's growing interest in youth culture. Mods had a few interesting revivals in the late '70s (the Jam and "This is the Modern World," Blondie with "Plastic Letters," and the Who's *Quadrophenia*), and later with the Two Tone explosion in the early '80s, along with the Fleshtones ("Roman Gods" and "Hexbreaker") and John Waters's film *Hairspray*.

Many Skins came out of the early '60s scene (via the sometimes-dubbed Hard Mod movement and the reluctance to become "climbers"—class-conscious). They also continued to evolve the youth ritual by following the Rude Bwoys, who not only introduced their style and attitude but their music—Rock Steady and, later, the Reggae music craze.

**5.** *Jerking the Modernist approach to distance, into "groovy times," is the dumbshow to the contemporary adoration of the absurdist tragic comedy = antiromantic. It presents itself, today, through the jaded situationism of talkshow culture. The sort that "Blast" and "Counter Blast" utilized through the headlines and print of newspapers. The newspapers place horror and glory side by side in a folio that has a calculated randomness. It will always assemble to state 1 thing = these events happen. It is only through such genres of media (music/comic/print/television), that we can see that each has a thing in common/coupons and advertising = rhetoric and metaphor. If the passage of a text takes on the sound and image of the disjointedness of casual speech and media, then the results are not only the coded tales being woven, but the presentation of the brutality that leads to the violent outcome.

**Monkey:** Monkey see, monkey do; monkey sometimes have BIG BIG FISTS and BODY. A person who just follows (see Bonehead, Stads, and Thug); a jock.

**Mugg (mug):** U.S. '20s–'30s gangster and street term for a face (my mug) or a hard worker (it's a mug's life); when one gets a "mug shot" taken he becomes a "mug," a term that changed to "wise guy" in the late '60s–early '70s. The phrases "mugging" for the camera, and "mugging" someone or getting "mugged" come from this.

The "mug" or "wise guy" or "soldier" is the street-level gangster, who does the work and gets his hands dirty for the higher, more privileged Mobsters. It's actually a cool term, mostly because of the gangster mythology in North America where they were and often are the urban outlaws and Mob bosses or Dons. Al Capone, Charles "Lucky" Luciano, Tony Accardo, and John Gotti are the most memorable alleged Mob bosses.

John Gotti was a hero because he was allegedly a "wise guy" who worked his way up from the street level and took over the privileged position of Mafia Don and remained loyal to his hood (as in *The Krays*). During the '80s, an era characterized by puritanical governmental intervention in the lives of individual citizens, Gotti emerged to defy authority—a muggish gentleman and a rebel against the system. He also wore great sharkskin suits.

It was during this era in which the term "mug" really started to change. Not too many people wanted to be a "mug" or "wise guy" until Gotti came along. Of course the *Godfather* saga helped too. Everybody wanted to be luey or Don. But too many Dons spoil the...

"Mugg" can be used in the same spirit as "thug." Depending on the context, it can mean a brainless tough or a bredda (as in "me and the muggs").

**No Means No:** Victoria, B.C., Canada band with a large cult following in North America. Noted for upsetting towns and police departments with their high energy concerts. Their music can't be easily defined.

**Odin's Law:** Fascist, WP band from Vancouver, B.C., Canada.

**Oi (or Oi yoi):** Adopted from the United Kingdom (lower-class) for hey. This term is the same as the Rude Bwoy call "yush." Depending on the intonation, it can signal anger, a call for attention, anger, a joyous greeting, or anger. Oi yoi is a slurred double greeting, French Canadian *joile*, used as an exclamation or for pain— often pronounced "I yoi," the same as in the screeching war cry (see **Wahling**). Also a North American sign of recognition/summoning/greeting from one Rudie/Skin to another.

Oi is also a form of sometimes melodic street punk that became popular with Skinheads in the late '70s and again in the late '80s and early '90s (see R.A.C.). A newer form of H.C.-influenced North American street punk is known as American Oi, a term taken from the compilation *US of Oi* (volumes one and two). Canada followed in spirit with its street punk release *Oi! Let's go...Canada!*

**Oxblood:** A New York City Oi band with an aggro, hypercool, street cult following. Also, a deep blood-red color often desired for Doc Marten boots or shoes.

**Ped(s):** Abbreviation for pedophile; a diddler (as in the Who's Evil Uncle Ernie); a user; a psychic vampire— the enemy.

**Perry, Lee "Scratch," and Gibbs, Joe:** Top producers and composers of Reggae and, especially, of an aggro form of Reggae that is, in more recent times, referred to as Skinhead Reggae (see Reggae).

**Pollack, Jackson:** American abstract expressionist artist, born January 28, 1912, died August 11, 1956, known for his violent, dark, emotional paintings, and his style of driving streaks of paint across a canvas by means of slashing or dripping the colors onto the surface, creating texture and emotional depth.

**Pork:** Oppression, unclean, a bad time, bad-minded people.

**Pricks, the:** A Victoria, B.C., Canada, drunk punk/street punk band with harsh vocals and lyrics filled with real sound bites from the lower parts of town. Noted for the Jaks Team affiliation and the bets made on whether or not they'll make it through a set. Decent music from guys who are what the Dead End Kids (a.k.a. Bowery Boys) would have sounded like if they had heard rock and roll and decided to picked up a guitar.

**Psychopathic G-d:** A cult book by Robert G. Waite that claims to offer a psychological profile of Adolf Hitler, his art, and the Thule Society.

**Puggugly:** From the Latin *pugno* meaning "battle" or "to fight." U.S. '20s–'30s gangster and street term for a rough person—a face that has seen a rough life or a lot of fists (as in actors Elisha Cook Jr. and Max Perlich).

**R.A.C. (Rock Against Communism):** A knee-jerk reaction to Rock Against Racism. The scene was founded, at least partially, by the National Front and Ian Stuart to entice young people into becoming political tools for a fascist cause. Also a minimalist form of Oi music influenced by Skrewdriver's (see **Stuart, Ian**) musical style. R.A.C. can be melodic, but usually has a simple rhythm and gruff vocals—almost Deathmetalish; the music is rhythm guitar driven. The lyrics are WP or influenced by the last NF, Pat Buchanan, or Reform Party rally.

**Rahowa (Racial Holy War):** A book by Ben Klassen. Also a band headed by Canadian racialist and creator of Resistance Records and magazine, George Burdi (aka George Eric Hawthorne), who nearly destroyed the North American Skinhead scene. Also, a late '80s and early '90s battle cry for North American WP conspiracy followers. The theory of race war is that there will be a final confrontation between Whites and anyone non-white, and that Whites will emerge victorious and claim final dominance over the earth (as in the philosophy of Charles Manson).

**Ratchet:** A jagged-toothed knife; term is used here interchangeably with "hatchet"; a small ax; a machete with a braided rope attached to give it a mobility and swing (as in Killer Pepé and the Ruff Riders/horde).

**Ratpatrol:** Based on the '60s TV show, a clean-up committee whose mission is to clear out treacherous blood in the neighborhood; violent confrontation of your oppressive forces as in Sam Peckinpah's ultraviolent western *The Wild Bunch;* a group of people banning together to fight an oppressive force (see Rude Bwoys).

**Reggae:** Poor people's music in the mid '60s to the very early '70s, not to be confused with the late '70s "Roots Reggae." A certain form of the music is also to referred as Skinhead Reggae, or, as Dave Barker and Ansell Collins put it, THE HEAVY MONSTER SOUND!— bashment, cool.

Skinhead reggae calls out to dance the night away and maybe even think about a few things. The beat (along with Ska, Rock Steady, and Punk) inspired Two Tone. With tunesters like the Hippy Boys, Clancy Eccles, the Upsetters, the Wailers, the Versitiles, the Pioneers, and the constantly evolving Maytals, Skinhead Reggae has become a soundtrack to a never ending lifestyle. The music is fast-paced to mid tempo, erratic, heavy on the bass, often experimental (influenced by Motown's excursions into recycled rhythm tracks, polyrhythms, and overdubs), witty, and filled with melodic vocals, dubs, shouts, and finger-mashing wacky keyboards.

**Rhygin:** (pronounced ri-gin) A term or title meaning rough, hypercool, feral, real hard. Also, Ivanhoe

"Rhygin" Martin, original Rude Bwoy (see Rude Boy/Bwoy) whose life was fictionalized in many Ska and Rock Steady songs and in the film *The Harder They Come,* starring Jimmy Cliff. A respected, hepster outlaw.

**Rock Steady:** Primarily the soundtrack for a Rude Bwoy from approximately 1964 to 1966. It is a slower and more complex form of Ska, and a version of what would become the hysterical Reggae rhythm. Its top producer is Sonia Portinger. The music is kept alive through contemporary U.S. bands like the Slackers, the Skanksters, the Hepcats, and the Jumpstarts.

**Rollins, Henry/Hank:** Publisher of *2.13.61* books. A big muscle guy with no neck and lots of tattoos who writes a lot and is always pissed off. He has a young, middle-class, often misguidedly angry male, and even a yuppie following. He is the former singer of Black Flag (starting from the "Damaged" full-length version).

**6.** *When a page is printed and screaming at you, it assumes the influences of the comic book, both visual and framed = Baddaboom Crash Crunch. The dadaist, after the end of one century and in the beginning of another, created sound poetry and newsprint collage. They conducted a guerrilla assault on the new industrial society and attempted to put an end to the purple passage and glamour and perfection of art.

**Rude Bwoy/Boy:** pl. Rudies (or Bad Boys, Bandolous,

Blackharts, Yush). Rebel, urban and social outlaw. A young male who is part of the outlaw brotherhood of Rock Steady- and Reggae-loving hooligans. Rude Bwoys are infamous for their habit of mashing up sound systems in rivaling dance halls. They are also famous for their shaved heads, sunglasses after dark, and hand-me-down, ankle-cut, ill-fitting (too-tight) pants—a point of gallant style for them and, later, for Skinheads. (For a comparison of U.S. and Jamaican Rude Bwoy style, see John Taylor's photography, especially "facing: Harlem Street Scene" in *Harlem USA #7*, edited by John Henrik Clarke, published in 1971.)

Rude Bwoys preceded and influenced the Skinhead in style and mettle. The Rude Bwoy roots are set in the very poor and run-down areas of Kingston and Trenchtown, Jamaica. The style then moved to England and, in various incarnations, to North America.

To most, Rude Bwoys were and are rebels, subverting the rules of poverty and European culture. They consisted of young Black men done in by colonialism, racism, and poverty. Fueled by their awe of American mobster gothic, spaghetti Westerns, and Afro-American revolutionary spirit and music, they made themselves a force to be reckoned with. The Desmond Dekker and the Aces song "007 (Shanty Town)" and Honey Boy Martin's boast on "Dreader Than Dread" provide examples of Rude Bwoy history and attitude.

These days the term and style are interchangeable

with Skinhead in the ranks of the Ska/Reggae scene, especially when the Skin shows a street savvy and/or is a *confrère* or bredda (as in tight crews such as "The Warriors," Culp and Cosby in *I Spy,* the Green Hornet and Kato, the James/Younger gang, and the Rat Pack).

It can be said that the modern-day equivalent of the Rude Boy/Bwoy is the Gangsta and the modern-day equivalent of the Skinhead is the Wigger. Rudies and Skins (Rude Boys/Bwoys) are used here as survivors, bluds, rebels, who would die for one another— they got each other's backs.

**Ruff Riders:** From the Rough Riders, the volunteer cavalry unit that fought in the Spanish-American War and charged up San Juan Hill under the leadership of Theodore Roosevelt, who became the 26th president of the United States of America. They were noted for their bravery and camaraderie. Also, harsh sex (riding the pony) and a song by Ska and Rock Steady king Cecil Bustamente Campbell (a.k.a. Prince Buster).

**Schmadda:** A Jew or a term used in the rag trade for cloth. Also, "Yud" [yood], from the German *Jüden.*

**Scott, Pastor:** Pastor Charles Scott (Chilliwack, B.C., Canada) of the Canadian Aryan National Arm—the Christian Identity Church of Christ in Israel and the Canadian division of the Posse Comitatus. Another A.N. affiliate is Terry Allen Long (Caroline, Calgary,

Alberta, and Creston, BC) who is former leader of the (Canadian) Aryan Nations.

**Sharkskin:** U.S. term for what is referred to in the United Kingdom as a tonik suit. It is made from flashy material that seems to reflect and change colour with light (as in *Miami Vice*). It was made popular by Jackie Wilson and Motown artists such as Jackie Wilson, the Temptations, and Smokey Robinson and the Miracles, and the Rat Pack (Sammy Davis Jr., Dean Martin, Frank Sinatra, Peter Lawford, and Joey Bishop), and later by "wise guys" in film and reality. Sharkskin is the favorite Friday/Saturday night or special events dress suit for cool, cool breddas and hooligans in general. The importance of this suit is that not only does it take a lot of dunza to get one, but once it's one your back, you can't help but say "Don't I look fucking sharp." Like Joe Pesci and Willy DeVille, it's real serious, stylin, THE SHIT!

**Shugaboo:** a Jamaican DJ exclamation made in the style of U.S. DJs Jocko Henderson and Wolfman Jack. Jocko and the Wolfman were the main influences on the stylin' DJ rap and boasts (along with Cassius Clay, better known as Muhammad Ali). It is used here as a term of endearment.

**Ska:** Jamaican R&B started in Kingston, Jamaica, in approximately 1962–63 by poor youths adapting the island sound and blending it with American Zydeco, Boogie Woogie, Jump, Doo-Wop, R&B, and, finally, Berry Gordy's Motown sound. It traditionally has a repeated hypnotic guitar riff and rhythmic horn section.

**Skanka/Skank/Skankin:** A trickster, thief, grifter, hustler; to trick or hustle someone; unclean. Also a dance imitating the early U.S. Apollo astronauts' walk on the moon. Usually done to Rock Steady or Reggae, the dance can involve a stationary, slick-motioned hop and skip. There is also a mock-aggressive, faster, "fists a-swinging" version with long strides forward in a circle—like a Hollywood Native American tribal war dance. This dance is now popular with the Ska, Reggae, H.C., and metal crowd. The Circle Jerks' "Kid Skank" is a good example of this version.

**Smackdead (eyes):** Term used for a junkie or ex-junkie who has developed a thin coat of haze over his eyes; a danger sign of a lost or dead soul.

**Snorky:** U.S. '20s–'30s gangster term for slick, cool dresser. Al Capone was referred to as being snorky. The same could be said the same for Edward G. Robinson, the Rat Pack, and John Gotti.

**Somebad:** Eastern Canadian (Nova Scotia) term meaning "real good," or used to emphasize the urgency of a point or desire.

**Specials, the:** From Coventry, England, they are founders of early 80s Two Tone label, cleverly mixing Punk, Ska, Rock Steady, and Reggae with football chant–style choruses. They combated the NF mentality and attempted to straighten out the dwindling Skinhead scene and lead the way in the return of Ska and the Rude Bwoy sensibility with a twist of logic. Along with the Selecters and the (English) Beat, they were pioneers in the realm of mixed-race bands and intelligent dance tracks.

**Spedderz:** Speed, crystal meth, crank.

**Squat:** A slum or abandoned building where street-level and/or homeless people live; a place to hang your hat; a possible home.

**Stad(s):** A "normal," upper- or middle-class person; someone going for status over style or individuality; part of the oppressive forces. The film *Repo Man* referred to stads as OFPs—ordinary fucking people. (A good example of stads are the "Socs" or "Socials," the rival gang to the "Greasers" in the S.E. Hinton book *The Outsiders*, published in 1967.)

**Steppinfetchit:** Afro-American early film actor Lincoln Perry's screen name. He was noted for perpetuating the stereotype of the dumb, slow, shuffling negro. Some Afro-American revisionists (such as playwright and director Ossie Davis) have looked on Perry's character as being very subversive and one of the forefathers of "work to rule."

**Stomperz, Moonstomperz:** A North American term for a Rude Boy or Skinhead who favors Ska, Rock Steady, and/or Reggae. Dance hits such as Warren Smith's "The Ubangi Stomp," The Flames' "Foot Stompin'," and the even more influential Reggae hit "Moon Hop" by Derrick Morgan helped open the floodgates for Symarip's classic "Skinhead Moonstomp." The US streetpunk band Rancid made the term popular with the anthem "Roots Radical" off the "Out Come the Wolves" release, as well as other songs.

**Stuart, Ian:** (deceased) Onetime lead singer of the R.A.C. (see R.A.C.) Oi band Skrewdriver. A treacherous figure known for bringing hate and the National Front (a British fascist party) to the Skinhead movement. His purpose was to seduce youths into being cannon fodder for the fascist cause. Skrewdriver's earlier releases are often praised (more so during the late '80s and early '90s in the United States) for their sound—dodgy. He almost singlehandedly brought the Skinhead scene to an end in the United Kingdom—a divisive force.

**Subway Thugs, the:** An Oi band from Vancouver, B.C., Canada. The band has an odd name, considering Vancouver has only have sky (elevated) trains.

**Swot/Swat:** A hard worker and/or (from SWAT— Special Weapons and Tactics) a street tough; someone who is heavy-handed, excessive in force, relentless, and often brutal.

**Templars, the:** A premier New York City American Oi band known for clever concept releases and stylin' tunes.

**Thug:** (from *Thuhgz, thuggee*); To conceal; Indian worshippers of Kali, stereotyped as ritual stranglers, with a colloquialism and subculture of their own, who would have the name tattooed under their bottom lashes. Now used in the same way as "Monkey" or sometimes as an exaggerated and possibly endearing term for someone who is prone to aggressive, smart-alecky behavior—rudeness.

**Urban Riot:** New York City American Oi band noted for their harsh music and brusque, socially relevant street lyrics.

**Vagenbwoyz:** Skinny, pale raver/twinky/teenage boy; often an extreme vegetarian with little brains.

**Van Cleef:** Lee Van Cleef, next to Clint Eastwood the top star of spaghetti Westerns such as *For a Few Dollars More* and *The Good, the Bad, and the Ugly*. His name was made even more popular when King Stitt recorded "The Ugly One (Van Cleef)".

**Ving, Lee:** Actor (*Dudes*) and vocalist on soundtracks such as *Alamo Bay*. Noted for his powerful voice and for being the lead singer of the pioneer San Francisco H.C. band Fear ("Have a Beer with Fear"). Often credited with introducing the American Skinhead look and attitude to North America. A real shit disturber. Best known for his appearance in *The Decline of Western Civilization* and for allegedly causing a riot (damage estimates ranged from $42 to thousands. See the January 1982 issue of *New York Rocker* and the November 3, 1981 issue of *New York Post*) on a Fear *Saturday Night Live* appearance after singing "Lets Have a War" from the band's first release, *The Record*.

**Wahling/Wailing:** Like a single prolonged "rebel yell," or like the Quebec *joile*, "[I] yoi" or "[I] yie" or "Woah Yoi" (see **Oi**); a Native American war cry—a sign of trouble (good or bad) and a warning to take cover. Also, to strike someone, to beat.

**Welly or wellybwoy:** Welfare or someone who works the welfare system (as opposed to having little choice but to be on it) rather than try to get out from under. Also, a player, a scrub (a male version of scrubber), user, or skanker (skanka)—a psychic vampire.

**Wigger:** "White nigger," Afro-American term for a White kid who adopts the oppressive dress, style, music, and language of Black ghetto youth.

**Wilson, Delroy:** The all-time best Reggae soul crooner. He stirs a sense of pride and revolution with "Beat Down Babylon," and is at his finest on the tune "Cool Operator."

**WP:** White Power/White Pride (White fascism).

**YDL:** Youth Defense League, an early U.S. Oi/street punk band from Brooklyn, New York, who sang "Skinhead 88," which boneheads seem to take too seriously.

**Zundel, Ernst:** Canadian publisher (Toronto) of Holocaust denial material and Jewish World Domination theory material. (See **Holohoaxer** and **Christie, Douglas.**

* from *5 mins. of Murder Alone (Texas)* 1994

## Music, Language and History References

*Conqueror Manifesto, The,* Helmkamp, Peter. G-d's Disgrace: Records & Publishing (Hyms of the Apocalypse), 1996.

*Dictionary of Caribbean English Usage, The.* Oxford University Press, 1996.

*Do A Runner!: Oi/Street-Punk 'Zine,* issues: 1-2, Lee69 (editor). Sound Views, 1997.

*Hardcore California: A History of Punk and New Wave,* Belsito, Peter and Davis, Bob (editors). Last Gasp of San Francisco, 1983.

*Kinder Nacht,* issues 1-5 1/2, Woles, Martin and Stewart, Scotty (editors). Island Easel, 1991-94.

*Lords of Chaos: The Bloody Rise of the Satanic Metal Underground,* Moynihan, Michael. Feral House, 1998.

*Maka: Diasporic Juks,* Douglas, Debbie; McFarlane, Courtney; Silvera, Makeda; and Stewart, Douglas (editors). Sister Vision, 1997.

*New England Hooligan,* issues: 1-2, Sims, Gordon (editor). Amherst, MA, 1997.

*Reel She Said,* issue 3 Notar, Clea (editor).

*Reggae: The Rough Guide,* Barrow, Steve and Dalton, Peter. Rough Guides Limited, 1997.

*Resistance Through Rituals: Youth Subculture in Britain,* Hall, Stuart and Jefferson, Tony (editors). Routledge, 1990.

*Skinhead,* Knight, Nick. Omnibus Press, 1982.

*Spear of Destiny, The,* Ravenscroft, Trevor. Samuel Weiser Inc., 1986.